After obtaining a BSc in Mathematics and Physics from London University, Robert Bradley qualified as a teacher and taught for six years in both England and Jamaica. Later qualifying as a chartered accountant, he joined the international mining company, Rio Tinto, and after 25 years working mainly in the UK and Canada, he took early retirement and became a freelance consultant for a number of banks and multinational companies in the USA and UK before returning to education.

A father of five children, he has written six books for his children and grandchildren, one adult novel, and numerous poems. This children's book, *Chocolate Robin,* is the first piece of writing he has submitted for publication.

GW00712314

To Abigail and Annabelle, Zohha and Zayb, Bojana and Owand, and Julen and Ana for all the encouragement they have given me, but especially to my wife, Vanessa.

c/o

Archie

Enjoy

Robert Bradley

5/3/20

rabradleyra@ hotmail. com

Robert Bradley

CHOCOLATE ROBIN

AUSTIN MACAULEY PUBLISHERS™

LONDON • CAMBRIDGE • NEW YORK • SHARJAH

Ordering Information:
Quantity sales: special discounts are available on quantity purchases by corporations, associations, and others. For details, contact the publisher at the address below.

Publisher's Cataloging-in-Publication data
Bradley, Robert
Chocolate Robin

ISBN 9781641824101 (Paperback)
ISBN 9781641824118 (Hardback)
ISBN 9781641824125 (E-Book)

The main category of the book — Fiction / General

www.austinmacauley.com/us

First Published (2019)
Austin Macauley Publishers LLC
40 Wall Street, 28th Floor
New York, NY 10005
USA

mail-usa@austinmacauley.com
+1 (646) 5125767

My thanks to Trevor Marlow of Marlow and Sons, Butchers.

Synopsis

On the death of his father, a young boy, Fred Smith, is sent to live with his aunt and uncle in 'a rundown shack', as Fred politely calls it.

Life at home is dominated by his eccentric uncle, who has become so large he is no longer able to get out of the main room. Fred's uncle dislikes the Smiths and makes things difficult for Fred. Shouting at him on his arrival and telling him he doesn't want him here, Uncle Victor leans so far out the window that he gets stuck. Extricating him proves difficult but highly amusing.

Fred strikes up an acquaintance with the scruffy Old English Sheepdog he saw in the lane when he arrived and, because of the large brown splodge on its white chest, he names it Chocolate Robin.

Together, they set off to find Fred's school. New to the area and joining in the middle of term, Fred is picked on and bullied. Having suffered this at other schools, he copes with the problem in a unique way: through his incredible sweets. The sweets are so good the leader of the bullies decides to make money selling them at school, but when he is caught he blames Fred, accusing him of bullying him into it. The head teacher punishes Fred by sending him home for a week.

Fred makes good use of the time. Unbeknown to his uncle, he begins cooking the evening meals and he and Chocolate Robin amuse themselves by rounding up a nearby flock of sheep to 'cut' the grass in the front garden.

During one night, Fred is awakened by a group of rats. Terrified and having no one else to talk to, the following day he tells Chocolate Robin what happened and is surprised when he comes home from school to find the barn owl that had started hanging about the garden appear with a few birds of prey and a couple of cats to drive out the rats.

Fred and Chocolate Robin make friends with a local butcher who encourages him to try to sell his sweets at the market. Unsure of how much to charge and worried that no one will want to buy them, it is not an easy thing for Fred to do and difficulties arise. He knows his sweets are good but that this is not enough; they have to be extra special, like nothing anyone has ever tasted before. An impossible task... or is it?

The following day, the barn owl starts draping sloppy strings of weed over the frame of Fred's bedroom window. Fred gets angry and decides to take it out on his uncle by cooking some of the weed and serving it to him, pretending it is cabbage. Instead of his uncle raving and shouting at him, as he usually did, he loves it. Is this the special ingredient he dreamt about? Will it change his life?

Chapter 1
Appletree Cottage

"It says it's the house on its own at the bottom of the lane… This must be it."

The social worker hesitated for a moment and turned towards the boy in her care, "It's called Appletree Cottage," she continued.

Appletree Cottage, thought Fred looking at the house in front of them, *Appletree Shack, more like it… And someone's run off with the apple tree!* But he remembered his manners and kept his thought to himself.

"I hope it never gets windy around here," said Fred.

The social worker turned and looked at him.

"It's not as bad as that," she replied, thinking he was upset at the sight of the unloved house with its overgrown garden and not realising he was trying to be funny.

Next to where Fred was standing, a rotten piece of wood with a few faded letters on it was buried in a clump of stingy nettles. He lifted his boot, kicked the nettles to one side, and then trampled them down far enough to be able to reach in with his hand. Trying desperately not to get pricked, he took hold of the sign between two fingers and carefully lifted it.

"Oops!" he said as it broke in his hand, "too many cornflakes for breakfast!"

"Don't worry, it wasn't your fault. If the owner complains, I'll tell him it was an unfortunate accident."

Ever since the social worker had collected Fred from the care home that morning, she'd been saying one nice thing after another to him. He'd tried to tell her she didn't need to and that he was alright, but nothing he did seemed to stop her.

He'd tried to make her laugh. He'd said silly things that couldn't possibly be true, like 'It isn't as if I'm going to live with an ogre,' but nothing seemed to help. Fred decided she was one of those grown-ups who thought 'jokes weren't meant to be funny'.

Gingerly putting the sign back where he'd found it, a movement caught Fred's eye. Just a few metres away from him, a scruffy looking Old English Sheepdog stood looking up at him.

"Hello, old boy," said Fred, guessing the dog was male but having no way of seeing through the straggly coat of hair dangling from the dog's back. "From your looks, I'd guess you live here?"

"WHAT DO YOU THINK YOU'RE DOING?"

A loud voice with the force of ten hurricanes boomed out from the direction of the house, almost knocking Fred and the social worker off their feet. The sudden noise scared them so much they instinctively wrapped their arms around each other and clung there like a couple of scaredy-cats frozen together on the school playground.

"AWAY WITH YOU!"

A moment of silence followed the two enormous outbursts of shouting. For some strange reason, the silence sounded more threatening and more deafening than the shouting itself.

"ARE YOU DEAF?"

Not yet, thought Fred, *but if you keep shouting like that, I will be soon.*

"GO AWAY, I SAID. DO YOU WANT ME TO GET MY GUN AND SHOOT YOU?!"

The social worker noticed she was clinging onto Fred and unwrapped herself. Shaking with fear, she grabbed hold of his hand to comfort him, but not knowing her own strength, she started to crush it. The effect was immediate: tears welled up in Fred's eyes and overflowed down his cheeks.

"Are you Mr. Floggit?" she squeaked, her words sounding like popcorn being shot out of her mouth. Still quivering with shock and without waiting for the man to reply, her tongue took over and started gabbling at a hundred miles an hour.

"We're looking for Appletree Cottage. The sign here… Oh, dear," she said and ground to a halt as she remembered what had happened to the sign.

"GO AWAY, I SAID," bellowed the enormous shape that appeared out of nowhere at the window, blocking the feeble light trying to escape from inside.

"I'm afraid we've broken your sign…" continued the lady. And not knowing what to say next but feeling she had to say something, her mouth took over again, "What I mean is I—"

"STOP BLATHERING, WOMAN!"

A smile crept across Fred's face. To anyone looking on from the outside, this might have seemed rude, as if he was making fun of the man. But it wasn't that. What was amusing Fred was that every time the man let out one of his shouts, the walls of the house shook violently, and the more

13

he shouted the more they shook; it was like watching slow-motion jelly wobbling on a plate.

A picture grew in Fred's head. *If we can keep him shouting,* he thought, *the house will fall down around him and he'll be left standing in the open air with the window frame dangling round his neck like a necklace.*

"GO AWAY, I SAID. IT'S NO BUSINESS OF YOURS WHO I AM. NOW AWAY WITH YOU. AND BE QUICK ABOUT IT."

To help pluck up her courage, the social worker gripped Fred's hand even more tightly than before, squeezing more tears out of his already-wet eyes and causing his knees to buckle.

"Mr. Floggit," said the lady, "you are Mr. Floggit?"

"HAVE YOU NOT GONE YET? I CAN'T STAND HERE ALL DAY TALKING TO YOU, I'M A BUSY MAN!"

If he thinks he's talking, I'd hate to hear him shouting! And as for being busy, Fred thought as he noticed that the huge man filling the window appeared to be wearing a sweater on top of what looked like his pyjamas, *it looks as if you've only just got out of bed!*

"I wrote to you last week," continued the social worker, releasing some of her grip on Fred's hand, reflating him back up off his knees onto his feet.

"In my letter, I informed you that you and your wife are the last known relatives of your brother-in-law Arthur Smith."

"WHAT'S THAT GOT TO DO WITH ANYTHING?"

"As his next of kin, you are now Fred's legal guardian, Mr. Floggit."

"NO. I. AM. NOT!" he screamed, pronouncing the words one at a time to make quite sure the lady heard them. "I REFUSEZzzz!"

The *Z* sound at the end of the word sped off across the grass in front of the house in Fred's direction. Narrowly missing him as it rushed through his hair, it leapt up over the hedge and set off down the lane to hide in the woods opposite.

In trying to hold on to the sound of the *Z* for as long as he could, the huge man's face began to turn redder, and redder, and redder. The entrance to the cave where his mouth once was became one giant sink-hole, opening and closing like a goldfish blowing bubbles in a bowl. But no sound was heard, for no noise escaped.

"Oh, dear," said the lady. "He's lost his voice," and, for the first time that day, she too was lost for something to say. She turned and looked at Fred, as if asking for help.

> *"When you're feeling sad or gay,*
> *Turn around, then smile and say*
> *Chocolate Robin!"*

he replied.

"Who taught you that?" she whispered.

"My dad. He said when things are not going well, saying that makes you feel better."

Fred held out his free hand to the social worker. "Here, give me both of your hands," he said, and, with their hands held together, they danced around and around in circles whilst Fred sang the words of his little poem.

"BE OFF WITH YOU, I SAID," screamed the man, who was by now half-hanging out of the window. "AND TAKE YOUR WAR DANCE WITH YOU!"

Chapter 2
Stuck

A high-pitched creaking noise penetrated the air. Stopping their dance and turning to see where it was coming from, Fred noticed the front door of the house slowly opening. With the gap barely wide enough for a kitten to squeeze through, the tiny head of a woman popped out and peered round the gap.

"Can I help you?" she mouthed, as if apologising for being there, "I'm Mrs. Floggit."

Surprised by the sudden appearance of a head without a body, Fred and the lady social worker turned and looked at each other.

"Chocolate Robin," said Fred and gave her a wink.

"THEY'RE NOT COMING IN HERE," shouted the ever-reddening face of the man who, like a volcano erupting into life again, was now overflowing the front window.

"Victor, please!" the woman pleaded.

The gentle sound of the woman's voice drew Fred's attention back towards the front door. The tiny head and shoulders of the woman making the noise reminded Fred of something he'd seen on the seafront last summer, but he couldn't quite remember what it was. And then it struck him. She looked like the head of one of the puppets from a Punch and Judy show that someone had stuck onto the end of a stick and was poking around the door.

"You must be the lady who's bringing Fred to live with us, now that my brother is dead?"

The woman's voice sprung into life again, surprising Fred, for he would have sworn her lips never moved.

"Yes, I am. And I've brought some papers for you to sign," said the care worker, trying to sound unafraid but failing miserably to do so.

Like a true gentleman, Fred stepped forward to open the garden gate to let the care worker into the garden and then hesitated. He decided it was best not to touch the gate, in case, like the house sign a few moments earlier, it might break off in his hand.

The gate—if it could be called a gate—looked as if it was permanently open and had been like that since before Noah built his ark. The only thing stopping it from falling over was a clump of long grass and a particularly large bramble.

Fortunately the gate was slightly open. Unfortunately, the bramble helping to hold it up had reached out its tentacles far enough to block the path.

"Let me go first your ladyship, in case it bites!" said Fred to the social worker and, with a few vigorous blows of his boots, proceeded to trample the bramble to the ground and kick it aside.

Having won the battle, the war was not yet over. Once past the gate, they had to fight their way through the jungle of long grass that guarded the house and blaze out a trail to the front door.

From time to time, Fred glanced, out the corner of his eyes, at the big blob hanging out of the window that was watching their every step.

On reaching the front door, Fred turned towards the social worker and whispered, "Don't look now, but I think the man's stuck in the window."

"Nora!" The voice of the red-faced man sounded anxious. The deep boom, which had begun to sound like a cross between a foghorn and a loud speaker about to blow up, had become more muted.

"Nora, come here! And be quick about it!"

Hearing the distress in her husband's voice, the lady's head disappeared inside the house as quickly as a tortoise's head pops into its shell at the first sign of danger. "I'm coming," she cried and the door squeaked shut behind her.

Fred and the social worker turned to see what was happening. The huge figure hanging out of the window was frantically wiggling and jiggling its arms in the air like a windmill caught in a surprise gale.

"As I thought," said Fred to no one in particular. "He is stuck."

"Hold onto my legs and pull!"

Fred presumed the man was talking to his wife, though it was hard to know for sure, as his head was in the garden and his wife was in the house.

With the man completely blocking the window, it was impossible to tell whether she was doing as she was told or not. All Fred could say for certain was his uncle didn't appear to have budged an inch, he looked well and truly stuck.

"Don't just stand there, you two. Can't you see we need help?"

I can see you need help, thought Fred, *my aunt looks alright to me!*

"Stop gawking and get over here and make yourselves useful."

Covering his mouth so his uncle wouldn't hear, Fred turned to the social worker, "How about you give him a push whilst I give him a pull? That way he'll be stuck there forever!"

"Hurry up," cried his uncle, "I can't stay here all day."

Fred thought of a good answer to that but wisely kept it to himself.

"We're coming," he cried and, pretending he was an explorer clearing a path through the jungle with a machete, set off towards the window.

"You wait until I get my hands on you, boy! Then we'll see who the funny one is! Now, get over here and push as hard as you can."

Fred and the social worker did their best to push the huge figure of his uncle back through the window, but it proved about as much good as trying to push a jelly fish through the eye of a needle. The harder they pushed, the further their hands buried into the fat of Uncle Victor's body and the more he spread out sideways onto the walls of the house.

In the end, Fred lost sight of his wrists and a good part of his arms as they disappeared into his uncle's mounds of flesh. For the sake of his life, he decided to give up. *If I push any harder, he'll swallow me up in one piece. I'll disappear inside him and be lost forever, like Jonah swallowed by the whale,* he thought.

"It's no good, Victor," squeaked Aunty Nora, whose voice somehow managed to squeeze its way past the blob blocking the window. "We'll have to call the fire brigade to get you out."

"YOU'RE NOT CALLING THE FIRE BRIGADE!" blasted the fog horn, bursting into life again.

Fortunately, the blast didn't last long. There was a brief pause and then it continued more quietly, "Have you forgotten I used to be a fireman? I'm not having my mates come round here laughing at me. Got any more bright ideas?"

"I could always get a shovel and try to dig you out," said Fred, trying not to laugh and backing away just far enough from the window to be out of reach of his uncle's arms as they tried to grab him.

"You wait 'til I get my hands on you," he cried, pulling his face tight and glowering at Fred.

The social worker stepped between the two of them. "I think you misunderstood what Fred was saying, Mr. Floggit. He was trying to be helpful."

"Helpful! When I get out of here, I'll show him how helpful I can be!"

"I've got an idea how he can escape," whispered Fred to the social worker. "If he stays there for a week without eating, he'll get thin and fall out all by himself."

"What are you two whispering about?" shouted his uncle. "Speak up, I can't hear you."

"I was just saying," said Fred, "if we rip—I mean, if we can get your sweater off, we might get you out of there."

Fred had no notion where the idea had come from and even less whether it would work, he just felt he'd gone too far in upsetting his uncle and it was time to mend bridges by trying to say something that sounded helpful.

"That's a good idea, Victor," came the muffled voice of his aunt as it found its way out of the house. She too had seen Fred was making a poor job of trying to help and was in danger of getting into serious trouble with his uncle. "It might work. There's no harm in giving it a try."

It was difficult for Fred and the social worker to hear what Aunty Nora was saying, for, with the window now completely blocked by his uncle's huge frame, the only way her voice could escape from the house was to force its way out through cracks in the walls or around the gaps in the woodwork.

There was a long moment of silence before Fred's uncle answered. "OK," he said, but it was obvious from his voice he wasn't convinced it would work.

Thinking back on it later, Fred would have loved to have had a camera to record what happened next.

First, the social worker took a pair of nail-scissors out of her bag and cut a hole in the woollen jumper his uncle was wearing on top of his pyjamas.

Then, it was Fred's turn.

He grabbed hold of the loose ends of the wool and gave them an almighty pull. Row by row, the sweater unravelled until all the bits of wool lay in a large heap on the grass.

"Now for the pyjama jacket," cried Fred, a little too gleefully for his uncle's liking, for it was obvious Fred was enjoying what he was doing more than he should have.

Rip, rip, tear, tear… tear, and rip. Fred couldn't ever remember having more fun in all his life. Shredding the last bit of Uncle Victor's pyjama top, he stood back to admire his handiwork… and wished he hadn't. For Uncle Victor— naked from the waist up, his fat ballooning out and cascading down in all directions like a waterfall hurtling towards the ground—was not a pretty sight.

"Right," said Uncle Victor, "now give it another go," obviously referring to the pushing and pulling and not the ripping and tearing; but no matter how hard they strained and pushed, Uncle Victor remained firmly stuck in the window.

"Any more bright ideas, clever clog?"

The obvious annoyance in his uncle's voice descended upon them.

Aunty Nora said nothing, because she knew Uncle Victor would explode if she did.

The social worker said nothing, because the only idea she had was to hire a crane to pull him out and she didn't think Fred's uncle would agree to that.

And Fred said nothing, because he was thinking.

"I know why you're still stuck," he said. "You're trapped in a vacuum. The air inside the house can't get out and the air outside the house can't get in. I'll have to make a hole so it can escape."

"YOU'RE NOT MAKING HOLES IN ME," shouted Uncle Victor.

Fred ignored the blast of noise bombarding his ears and shut his mind to the picture of Uncle Victor looking like a smelly cheese with lots of holes in it.

"Don't worry, Uncle, I'm not going to make a hole in you," he said, deliberately calling him uncle by name for the first time in the hope it might calm him down. "Trust me."

"Trust a Smith! I've never trusted the Smith family in all my life and I don't see why I should start now!"

"But, Victor, I think it's a good idea. Let the boy try."

"Let him try, let him try! It's me, not you, that's stuck in this window."

Hey ho! thought Fred. *Here goes. Let's face it, I can't get into any more trouble than I am already in.* And, with that, he stepped forward to the window reached up with both hands and burrowed them deep into the fat of Uncle Victor's enormous stomach.

"This had better work, boy. Or you're in trouble."

In no time at all, Fred's arms were almost completely buried under the squidgy, quivering mass of his uncle's blubber and yet there was no sign of the window frame. He tried not to think about it, but his head was now only inches away from his uncle's belly button.

Desperate to find the window, he wiggled and woggled his fingers further and further under his uncle's flesh until the side of his face pressed up against his uncle's skin and he started having difficulty breathing.

Desperate times call for desperate measures! And, with that, he shut his eyes and buried his head deep into his uncle's stomach.

Like a busy beaver tunnelling, Fred ploughed his way through mound upon mound of fat to reach the window frame before he died in the attempt. Wishing he had one hand free so he could clamp his nose, all he could do was hold his breath and hope not to be suffocated by the stink.

After what seemed like eternity and with his lungs bursting for breath, his fingers touched the wood surrounding the window.

Now for the difficult bit, Fred thought.

Pushing his fingers up and over the ledge of the window, he broke the air gap. A sudden rush of warm, smelly air erupted past him, followed a moment later by a loud, disgusting noise that his dad would have told him off for if he'd been there to hear it.

The vacuum was broken.

The foundations of the house began to shake and Uncle Victor's body shot backwards through the window like a space rocket. A dull, squishy sort of sound followed as he splatted onto the wall behind and fell to the floor like a soggy sack of seaweed dropped from a great height.

Whoa, didn't know walruses could move that quickly, thought Fred as he gasped for breath.

Chapter 3
The House

After all the excitement was over, Fred and the social worker made their way back to the front of the house and waited for Aunty Nora to come to the door.

It took a long time, and thinking she'd forgotten all about them, they were about to knock on the door when it creaked open and Aunty Nora's head popped out through the narrow opening.

She twisted her neck and peered at them.

"You have something for me to sign?" she inquired.

The social worker and Fred stepped back to let Aunty Nora open the door a bit wider so they could go inside, but nothing happened.

"You have some papers for me to sign?" she repeated, thrusting a wizened arm out and around the door.

The sudden movement startled Fred. Imagining a Moray eel emerging from its hole at the bottom of the sea and moving forward to bite him, he jumped backwards. Instinctively, he turned towards the social worker for help but saw that she too was scared and didn't know what to do. Like a rabbit caught in the headlights of a car, she was frozen to the spot.

"The papers?" said Aunty Nora.

With a zombie-like stare on her face, the social worker reached into her bag and rummaged inside. She took out a handful of papers, tentatively passed them to the bony tentacle twitching in front of her, and pulled her hand back quickly, as people do when feeding a horse.

The papers, the tentacle, and Aunty Nora's head disappeared as one inside the house and the door creaked shut behind them.

Nonplussed, Fred and the social worker stood together in silence until Fred, not knowing what else to do, started to recite his Chocolate Robin poem and they both laughed.

Moments later, a murmuring noise could be heard from inside the cottage. Inaudible at first and hard to make out, as time went on the sound grew louder and louder. The last words they heard were, 'Well, I'll have nothing to do with him. Never did like your family. I don't want him here, I tell you'.

"I hope they've got a dog," said Fred.

The social worker appeared not to hear what Fred said or, if she did, didn't know what to reply.

"I've always wanted a dog," he continued, undeterred, and turned to look at the social worker. He could see that her mind was elsewhere.

"You'd need a big dog if you lived here," he continued, deciding to resume his conversation with himself. "And I mean a big one, a little one would get lost in the jungle," he said, pointing at the long grass that must, once upon a time, have been a front garden.

Fred broke off his monologue as the cottage door creaked open and Aunty Nora's head reappeared, her arm clutching the bundle of papers.

"We've signed them," she said.

The social worker took the papers and, accepting she was not going to be invited inside, sat down on the ground to read them. One by one, she turned the pages checking that each had been signed correctly.

"They look to be in order," she said and stood up to give Aunty Nora her copy.

What happened next happened so quickly not even Fred had time to react. The ghostly figure of Aunty Nora came out of the house, grabbed her copy of the papers, and, taking hold of Fred's arm, pulled him with her into the house through the narrow opening in the door.

"Excuse me, Aunt Nora, but I haven't said thank you to the lady who brought me here."

He turned to go back outside and realised from the darkness that his aunt had closed the door behind them. Unable to see clearly, Fred reached out his hand and groped his way back towards the door.

Eventually, he found the handle. It was an old-fashioned one that opened by lifting a catch. He placed his shoulder against the door, pressed down on the lever, heard the noise of the latch opening, and gave the door a push.

Nothing happened. The door refused to budge. He placed his shoulder hard against it and gave it a hefty shove. It opened a fraction, but no more than a few inches; not enough even for someone as small as him to squeeze through.

He took a step back, lowered his shoulder, and charged.

Two things happened: he hurt his shoulder and the door opened just wide enough for him to slide around.

Outside on the grass, the social worker was trying to put her copy of the papers back into her bag and catching flies with her open mouth as she did so.

"I wanted to say goodbye and to thank you," said Fred, noticing she looked perplexed.

It was the social worker's job to see that Fred would be properly looked after, and the fact that she'd heard his uncle shouting that he didn't want his nephew to stay with them was not a good sign. She had the right to knock on the door and insist on going inside, but she was too frightened to do it.

"Everything will be alright," said Fred, as if he could read the thoughts going through the social worker's mind. He bent down and picked up the small suitcase containing the few things he had left in the world.

"I wanted to wish you a 'Chocolate Robin'."

"Oh," she said. "Oh, it's you, Fred," and she gave him a smile. "And a 'Chocolate Robin' to you too!"

Deep in thought, she paused for a moment.

"Are you sure everything will be alright…?" she asked and, without waiting for an answer, set off through the long grass in the direction of the garden gate.

Fred watched her leave and waved to her as she walked off down the lane and out of sight.

He turned and went inside. His first thought was to go to the window to wave a final goodbye, but it was so dark inside he wasn't sure he'd find his way across the room without tripping over something and making a fool of himself.

"We really must do something about this door, Victor," said Aunty Nora, breaking the silence by slamming it shut. "It won't open or close properly."

"Then mend it, dear Nora, dear Nora, dear Nora. Then mend it!"

* * * *

After the brightness of the sunshine outside, Fred could see nothing in the darkness inside. Frightened he might be attacked, he held his suitcase in front of him like a shield.

"Say hello to Uncle Victor."

Fred had no idea from which direction his aunt's voice had come and, try as hard as he could, it was so dark inside he had no idea where his Uncle Victor was either.

I've gone blind, he thought.

Much as an owl does, he scrunched his eyes shut, counted to three, and re-opened them. But, unlike an owl, which has no problem seeing in the dark, Fred still had no idea where Uncle Victor was.

"What's the matter with the boy? Is he blind or something?"

Fred could tell from the voice that his uncle was enjoying himself.

"Have ants got your tongue boy? Have the fairies run off with it?"

In all of his life, Fred had never been afraid of the dark. He didn't believe in 'boogie men' or 'ghostie things', but he did like to see what was in front of him, where steps and obstacles were, or holes might be. He was terrified now, for he had no idea where his uncle was or what he might do next.

"Say hello to Uncle Victor," repeated Aunty Nora.

Fred backed himself up against the wall next to where he'd come in and made himself as small as possible behind his suitcase. He took a deep breath to give himself courage and then turned to face where he thought Uncle Victor's voice had come from.

"Hello, Uncle Victor," he said to what he later found out was a hat and coat stand.

"Don't you hello me,' shouted his uncle. "And look at me when I'm talking to you!"

I'd love to, thought Fred, *but I've no idea where you are. How can anyone as big as you go missing in a room as small as this. You must be the world champion at hide and seek.*

"YOU'VE RUINED MY BEST SWEATER," shouted Uncle Victor, turning the volume up a notch, "AND MY PYJAMAS," he added as an afterthought.

Now that his uncle was shouting, Fred worked out from which corner of the gloom the noise was coming and focused his eyes in that direction. Little by little, they adjusted to the light, and delighted to find he was no longer blind, he stopped himself from crying out 'Uncle Victor! I can see your fat glowing in the dark,' and smiled instead.

"He's as stupid as all the Smiths," said Uncle Victor, a bit short of breath after his last outburst. "Now let's get one thing clear from the start…"

He paused for effect.

"This is my room…"

He paused again.

"And I don't want to see you in here again. Do you hear me?!"

"But, Victor," said his aunt, "he has to come through the room to get in and out of the front door."

"No he doesn't. He can use the back door!"

"But we haven't got a back door, Victor."

Logic was obviously not one of Uncle Victor's strong points. Set back by his wife's words, it took him a few moments to collect his thoughts again.

"There's a window in the attic, he can use that to get in and out of the house. Now stop arguing, woman, and get me some clothes, do you want me to sit here half naked all day and catch my death from cold?"

Now there's an idea, thought Fred.

A dim shaft of light on the far side of the room told him that Aunty Nora was leaving the room to get Uncle Victor's clothes and he used the opportunity to take a quick look around. And it was a quick look, for the room was tiny.

Apart from the hat and coat stand he'd just said hello to, the only things he could see in the room were a small table and two chairs; oh, and Uncle Victor of course. Fred guessed there was another piece of furniture and that it was probably a sofa, but it was only a guess, for it was impossible to see. Uncle Victor was sitting on it.

Sitting was the first word that came into Fred's head, but it was perhaps not the best one to use; 'filling it,' 'completely filling it,' 'overflowing it,' 'smothering it,' or 'killing it' might all have been better. For the first time in his life, Fred felt sorry for a piece of furniture. Uncle Victor was so fat his body bulged up over the arms of the sofa and flowed down onto the floor like lava out of a volcano.

"And what do you think you're looking at, boy?" shouted Uncle Victor. "I'll give you something to look at if you're not careful."

There were two doors into the room. They were ordinary doors, such as you get in any house. Then, there was his uncle; far from ordinary and certainly not something you get in any house.

I understand why Uncle Victor says it's his room, Fred thought, *the doors leading in and out are too small for him to get through! He's trapped inside.*

Fred's mind went into overdrive at the thought of his uncle being trapped inside forever, and the words of a little song formed in his head:

> *Stuck inside*
> *Far too wide*
> *There's nowhere at all he can hide.*
> *He'd love to go walking*
> *Instead of just talking*
> *But he can't 'cos he's all stuck inside.*

Tempted to start humming it, he didn't dare for fear of what might happen if he did. He glanced at his uncle and a silly idea came into his head. He imagined him going out for a walk.

'I'm just going for a walk, Nora. You don't mind if I take the house with me, do you?'

And he pictured the house walking off down the lane with Uncle Victor inside, carrying it with him... And, standing where the front door had been, Aunt Nora waving goodbye and saying, "Don't be long, Victor. It looks like it's going to rain and I don't want to get wet."

Aunty Nora hurried back into the room carrying Uncle Victor's clothes under her arm. She was in such a hurry the draft created when she pushed the door open blew some of the stale air in the room in Fred's direction. The sudden pong wiped the smile off his face. *Goodness me! If it smells like this when we've been opening and shutting the doors, what must it smell like if they're closed all day?*

"THIS IS ALL YOUR FAULT, BOY," shouted Uncle Victor, who, with Aunty Nora's help, was trying to do the impossible and climb into his clothes.

"You've only been here five minutes and already you've cost me a fortune. That was my favourite jumper you tore to pieces... Not to mention my pyjamas!"

Fred didn't answer, for he knew anything he said would only make matters worse. And, at any rate, something was troubling him. It was something to do with the furniture, but he didn't know what.

Then, suddenly, like the smell in the room a few minutes ago, it hit him.

There was no toilet in the room for Uncle Victor to use. If he's trapped inside the room, where does he go when he wants the toilet?

Chapter 4
Fred's Bedroom

There was a brief moment of silence that didn't last long. Having bullied his wife into helping him dress, Uncle Victor suddenly changed his mind and shouted at her to leave him alone, for she'd hurt him as she pulled his sweater down over his head.

Through the gloom across the room, Fred was barely able to make out what was going on, but he soon realised that his uncle had made another bad decision. For the second time that day, he'd managed to get himself stuck; this time inside his sweater. Waving his arms outstretched above his head and gyrating them in all directions, he was trying to find the openings to the sleeves; he looked like a beached walrus wallowing in the waves.

"Come with me," said Aunty Nora, drawing Fred's attention away from his uncle's antics. Her voice harsh and cold.

Protected by the hat stand next to him and the suitcase he was clutching firmly in front of him, Fred was reluctant to follow her.

"Your room is in the attic!"

This is my chance to escape, he thought, and with all the enthusiasm of a cat thrown out into the rain, he plucked up his courage and sidled his way past his uncle.

He got as far as the door, but no further. Tiny though she was, his aunt was having difficulty squeezing past a ladder that was blocking her way. Fred peered over her to see if he could help but realised there was nothing he could do. In front of the door was the most miniscule of spaces he'd ever seen. It was supposed to be a hallway, but it was so small that only the tiniest of contortionists could feel comfortable in it.

"Your room is up there," said his aunt, pointing vaguely upwards in the direction of the ceiling.

Trying not to lean on her and squash her, Fred bent forward and twisted his head to look up. He felt his eyes drawn like iron filings to a magnet as they hopped from rung to rung up the ladder towards a cave-like hole overflowing with darkness.

He felt the air trapped inside pressing down on him. He could only guess what might lie up there, and from the ramshackle state of the house and the garden, he was in no hurry to find out.

He looked away and turned his attention, instead, to the three doors he could see in front of him. Each one was open.

Through the one on his left was a kitchen. Tiny, like the rest of the house, it was barely big enough to turn around in.

Through the one on his right, a wash-hand basin and toilet sat huddled so close together they were either good friends or frightened of something.

The third door, the one directly in front of him, was only open a fraction. He guessed it led into Aunty Nora's bedroom and, because so far he'd seen no sign of a bath, he hoped that might be in there too. But how could that be possible? From the size of the other rooms in the house, there would not be enough room for both a bed and a bath to be squeezed into so small a space; unless, of course, his aunt used the bath as her bed!

Without needing to move her feet or leave the living room, his aunt reached out one of her thin arms and groped around the door into the kitchen.

"Here," she said and handed him a candle and a box of matches, "you'll want these."

Fred tried to hide his look of surprise.

"There are no lights in the attic," she said in answer to his look.

"Oh," he replied and swallowed the words 'that's nice' as they arrived on his lips.

Unsure of what he was expected to do next, he waited for his aunt to say something, but, when nothing came, he decided that was the end of her explanation. He tucked the candle and matchbox under the arm carrying his suitcase and with his free hand grabbed hold of the ladder.

"Be careful!" said his aunt when he was halfway up.

Fred stopped. He waited for her to tell him what he had to be careful about, took the time to check if there were rungs missing on the ladder, saw there weren't, counted to ten, and continued on his climb.

"Be careful not to set fire to the house…"

Just before he reached the opening into the attic, he fished the candle and box of matches out from under his arm, lifted his suitcase up above his head and placed it down onto the floor of the attic. He pushed it far enough away from the ladder, so as not to trip over it, and, with his head below the opening and his feet firmly planted on the rungs, ready to flee, he took a match out of the box to strike it.

"Do you have a watch?" called out his aunt.

Do I have a watch? he thought. *What's a watch got to do with lighting a candle? Surely she doesn't want me to use the candle as a clock? Doesn't she know they stopped using candles as clocks hundreds of years ago?*

"You might be able to see the town hall clock from up there?"

Fred had had enough of listening to his aunt going on about time, watches, and town hall clocks and concentrated, instead, on lighting the candle. But the tension was getting to him. His hand shook so much he failed to light the candle on the first attempt and blew out the match before the flame burned his fingers. He took out another match but dropped it.

"…or perhaps not?" she continued. "It's years since anyone's been up in the attic."

Now that his aunt had started talking, she didn't seem to be able to stop… "You used to be able to see the town hall clock from up there… Perhaps trees will have grown in the way by now?"

The idea that no one had been up into the attic for years was the last thing Fred wanted to hear. His aunt's words filled him with dread. *What was up here? Would it be infested by bats… feral cats… packs of rats?* To take his mind off the thought, he tried to light the next match but dropped that one too. *Perhaps the tigers we didn't see in the garden sleep up here!*

Overcome by fear, Fred clung to the ladder and his feet froze to the rung. He could neither go up nor down. And yet, somehow, he had to see what was up there; something was drawing him on.

He took out another match and was about to strike it when a thought struck him. He'd seen a window in the attic when he first arrived at the cottage. It was the middle of the day; he might not need the candle.

He squinted his eyes and peered into the gloom above him. He knew it was a lovely day and the sun was shining outside, but there was no sign of its light penetrating the darkness inside the attic. There had to be a window. Hadn't Uncle Victor said Fred should get into and out of the house through the window in the attic? But where was it? It couldn't have disappeared.

A new wave of panic flooded over him; a feeling there was no way out, that he was trapped. A cold sweat broke out on his brow. A trickle of moisture ran down his forehead onto the bridge of his nose.

Perhaps Uncle Victor's hung a blanket over the window for when he practises his hide and seek, he joked. *Or perhaps, if I'm lucky, the tigers will share some of their food with me?*

The thought of Uncle Victor and sharing the tigers' food made Fred's tummy rumble. He turned to call down to his aunt to ask what time lunch would be, then changed his mind. To cheer himself up, he'd walk into town and buy something there. Cheeseburger and chips sounded good; covered with ketchup, lots of ketchup. His mouth began to water.

"A Chocolate Robin to anyone who's hungry," he said and he imagined his teeth sinking into the cheeseburger, its juices spilling over the sides of his mouth and dribbling down his chin.

Chapter 5
Inside the Attic

Fred heard the shuffle of his aunt's feet as she turned and stepped back into the front room and the noise of the door closing behind her. Seconds later, Uncle Victor's voice wound up to its normal volume.

"He's not having his meals in here."

"But, Victor, he has to." Like a warrior preparing for battle, his aunt's voice rose in unison with her husband's.

"No, he doesn't. He can eat up stairs."

"But, Victor, there's no table and chair up there."

"So?"

"Victor, be reasonable, let him at least have breakfast down here… Before he goes to school… And he doesn't know where the school is… We have to tell him how to get there… We…"

Each phrase she uttered was broken by a pause, as if she were looking at her husband, pleading with him. And each phrase was spoken with increasing intensity, as if she thought the louder she spoke the more likely she was to convince him to agree with her. Then, as suddenly as it had started, her voice trailed off like an echo blown in the wind. Fred could tell she'd lost the argument; given up.

The intense flash of light as the match lit and burst into life made Fred shut his eyes. He waited a few moments for them to adjust, then held the match up against the wick of the candle. He watched mesmerised as it coughed and sputtered, gathering its strength to spread its light across the room to do battle with the darkness.

The candle lost!

Too feeble to penetrate more than a metre, its light was quickly smothered by a thick wall of cobwebs, making it impossible for Fred to tell how big the attic was. The only thing he could see was the light rapidly dulling as it tried to spread out into the darkness. It was impossible to tell where the light from the candle ended and the darkness in the attic began. It was like sitting on a beach looking out to the horizon and never finding the line where the sea ended and the sky began.

"Lord Fred," he said, putting on yet another of his brave faces. "Lord of all you survey!"

With the candle held high above his head, he climbed the rest of the way up the ladder and stepped onto the floor of the attic with about as much confidence as if he were landing on an alien planet. To cheer him up and bring him luck, he mumbled a quick 'Chocolate Robin' and crossed the fingers on both of his hands before setting off to explore the farthest reaches of his kingdom. He'd have crossed his toes if he hadn't needed them to walk on.

In no time at all, Fred was covered in cobwebs and dead spiders, and in no time at all, he was touching the walls of the attic. It was only by chance he stumbled across the window he was looking for. It was no wonder he'd not found it earlier, for it was covered in so much dirt and grime that any light brave enough to try to pass through died in the attempt.

Now where's my bed?

But try as he did, he found no sign of his bed, for if the truth was known, there was nothing to be found; no table, no chair, no cupboard. Apart from the cobwebs, the spiders, and the dust, the attic was empty.

Fred sat down on the floor, put his head in his hands, and did his best not to cry.

> *"When you're feeling sad or gay*
> *Turn around, then smile and say*
> *Chocolate Robin!"*

It was all he could do to pick himself up. He swiped as many handfuls of cobwebs and dead spiders off his clothes and hair as he could and trudged the one or two steps needed to reach the ladder. At the pace of a dried-up snail, he climbed down and, mustering all the courage he could find, cleared his throat and knocked on the living room door.

"IT'S THAT BOY AGAIN. HASN'T HE GONE TO BED YET?"

"That's the problem," said Fred, who, on hearing his uncle shouting at him, raised his voice in frustration, "I haven't got a bed."

Like popcorn fired from a gun, Fred's aunt's head appeared at the doorway, startling him.

"You mustn't upset your uncle by shouting."

Her voice too was raised, but Fred could feel that she, unlike his uncle, didn't mean it and was perhaps only speaking loudly like this to convince her husband she was on his side. But, by now, Fred was past caring why she was doing it. He'd had enough of adults playing their silly games. He was angry. He wanted his uncle to hear how he felt about things.

"Tell me, Aunty," he said, and the words that followed next flowed out of his mouth like a torrent of water over a waterfall.

"Are walruses frightened of mice? I know elephants don't like mice. Do mice trumpet like elephants? Is it mice in the house that I can hear, or are they walruses? I haven't seen any mice in the house but I have seen an…"

Before Fred could finish his sentence and start what would certainly have been a full declaration of war against his uncle, one he could not have won, his aunt slipped out of the front room and, like a ghost appearing in the night, was standing between Fred and the living room door, which she'd somehow closed quietly behind her.

"Now, what was it, Fred?"

The tone of her voice was gentle and caring; her eyes reassuring. The avalanche of snow that had fallen on Fred's head melted around him

"Aunty Nora, I don't have a bed to sleep on."

Fred spoke slowly and with a calmness that surprised even himself. He'd had enough of fighting. He'd had enough of shouting. He'd had enough of everything. He just wanted a bed.

"Oh!" she replied. "Oh!"

Fred closed his eyes. *Please don't tell me I've not got a bed to sleep on!* he thought.

"Oh, Fred, I'm sorry. I knew there was something I'd forgotten."

She squeezed her way past the bottom of the ladder and pushed open her bedroom door. Except for her bed and a small wooden cupboard, the room was empty; there was no sign of a bath.

Aunty Nora bent down and picked some things up off the floor: a pillow and small bundle of bed clothes, on top of which sat a blue square of plastic.

"The blue thingamabob on top is your mattress. You blow it up."

'Blow it up! It looks like it's been blown-up... Exploded... Got a hole in it... Flattened,' he wanted to say, but he kept his mouth shut. He'd had enough of trying to be funny just to amuse himself. Being funny didn't seem funny anymore.

"Can I have something to eat?" The words blurted out of his mouth before he could stop them.

"Ah!" said his aunt, which made a change from her saying 'Oh', "I did have some food for you. I left it out on the living room table. I was going to bring it up to you when you'd settled in, but..."

She turned her eyes away and looked down at the floor, "...but your uncle's eaten it."

"I'll take that as a no then!" said Fred, forgetting his manners as his anger rose again and bubbled out over his lips.

"I could spare a slice of bread if that will do until tomorrow? But I'm afraid you can only have one slice; we need the rest for breakfast."

As she searched for her words, his aunt's eyes scoured the floor like radar looking for bread crumbs. "It's too late to go to the shops now."

'Too late? Too late! It can't be too late, it's the middle of the day,' was what he wanted to say, shout it even, but what was the point, for he'd guessed by now what his aunt was trying to tell him. He could see it written on her face, in the garden, in the house. His aunt and uncle were poor. He was poor. They came from a poor family.

"I think I'll go out for a walk, Aunty," he said, "to enjoy the sunshine."

He turned and made his way back up the ladder, clutching his bundle.

"Don't worry, Aunty," he said to himself when he reached the top. "Don't worry, everything will be alright. You'll see."

Chapter 6
Chocolate Robin

Fred dropped the inflatable mattress and the bedding into a heap on the floor of the Attic and watched the dust fly up into the air and smother the candle.

"Come on, little fella," he said as he picked it up off the floor before its flame died.

He cupped his hand around the wick to protect it and waited for the flame to flicker back to life.

"What do you say we team up? You attack the gloom and I fight the spiders!"

Fred tried not to think about how many creepy-crawly creatures were lurking in the cracks and crevasses of the attic, waiting to pounce on him. He could see this was their home. For years, they'd crawled unhindered, criss-crossing the space between the ceiling and the floor, covering it with their sticky webs. It was like an untamed jungle.

He put his head down and, in much the same way as earlier in the day when he'd attacked the long grass in the front garden, he swiped and hacked his way towards the point in the room where he thought the window was.

The faint glow of light passing through the grime and dust as he approached led him to it, but it was impossible for him to see out because of all the layers of dirt and grime caked on its panes.

He chose what he thought was the least dirty pane and set about cleaning it, but not having a bucket of soapy water, or indeed water of any sort, all he could do was use his spit and clean it off with the only piece of material he had at hand: the sleeve of his shirt.

His efforts quickly developed into a game of mud pies. The dirt was so thickly encrusted on the glass that, in no time at all, the marks left behind by his cleaning resembled swirling tyre tracks in a farmer's field. Fast running out of spit and still unable to see out, he gave up and tried to open the window instead, only to discover that, like the garden gate, it was hanging on by a wish, a thread, and a few cobwebs.

Taking care it didn't come off in his hand and crash down into the garden below, he pushed it open as far as he felt it would go without breaking. He climbed up onto the ledge and sat there with his feet outside and looked around him.

The town clock his aunt had talked about was nowhere to be seen. There was no sign of tigers roaming in the long grass either. The only thing of note was the garden gate. Hanging from its hinges with its mouth open, it looked up at him in wonder at what he was doing sitting up there.

I hope Uncle Victor's right and there is a ladder in the garden. I'll never be able to climb back in without it and the last thing I want to do is to have to knock at the front door and set the elephant off trumpeting again.

A sudden movement in the lane caught Fred's eye. A large, shaggy dog with dirty, long, white hair coloured with brown splodges here and there was ambling along as if it owned the place. It was the same dog Fred had talked to on his arrival.

The dog stopped what it was doing and looked up.

"I don't wish to be rude," Fred called out, "but there's a big, brown splodge on your chest that makes you look a bit like a puffed-up robin!"

The dog didn't seem the least bit interested.

"Hang on a minute," called Fred, "I'm coming down. Don't run off."

In his haste to slide gently down the roof and land in the long grass in the garden, Fred didn't notice the roof was covered in moss and, as he set off, his foot slipped. Instead of a nice, two-legged, controlled slide down the short stretch of tiles, he was twisted over onto his side. And before he had time to straighten up his feet, he'd reached the edge of the roof.

To stop his descent, he thrust the sides of his shoes into the gutter and, to his relief, came to a halt.

The gutter held his weight. But it was only for a moment. With a loud crack, it suddenly broke and Fred tumbled out of control over the edge of the roof. He made a desperate lunge at the passing drainpipe and managed to grab it and hold on.

"Phew that was lucky!"

But it wasn't as lucky as he first thought, for, inch by inch, the pipe pulled away from the wall under his weight and, like the pole-vaulter who forgot to let go of his pole, he crashed onto his back into the long grass of what had once been a flower bed.

The force of the fall knocked all the wind out of him. With stars flying around in his head, he lay on the ground in pain gazing up at the sky, its blueness reminding him of the colour of his dad's eyes.

"I miss you, Dad! I wonder what it was you wanted to tell me before you died."

And he recalled his father's last words.

'You know the poem… the one called Chocolate Robin? There was something I didn't tell you.'

At this point, his dad had paused for he was desperately tired.

'I want you to listen carefully…'

But these were his father's final words.

* * * *

"WHAT'S ALL THAT NOISE OUT THERE?"

"Is that a walrus I hear singing a love song from afar?" said Fred, cupping a hand to his ear mimicking someone trying to detect a faint noise far in the distance.

"NORA, HE'S BROKEN SOMETHING! YOU WAIT UNTIL I GET MY HANDS ON HIM. I'LL GIVE HIM SUCH A BEATING."

Uncle Victor sounded even more angry than he did when he and the social worker had arrived an hour or so earlier. Fred had to admit he'd been frightened then, but he wasn't frightened now, for he knew his uncle couldn't get out of the living room to do anything to him.

Even so, he didn't want to wait around to find out.

Ignoring the pain from his fall, he picked himself up off the ground and, as best he could, ran out through the garden gate and into the lane.

"Hello, boy," he said as he bent down to give the dog a friendly pat.

But the dog had other ideas. Jumping up onto its hind legs, it landed its huge paws on Fred's shoulders and planted a great, big, slobbering wet lick full on his face.

"You're about as dirty as my attic," said Fred to what he could now see was an enormous Old English Sheepdog. "If that's possible?" he added as he tried to wipe the dog's slaver off his face.

"WHERE DO YOU THINK YOU'RE GOING, BOY?"

Uncle Victor, who'd turned up the volume on his foghorn to super-mega blaring mode, had somehow managed to lift himself off the sofa for the second time that day and was poking his head out of the front window.

Fred turned to the dog.

"This could be fun. If we can get my uncle worked up enough, he might lean out of the window and get stuck again. What do you say we give it a try?"

The dog didn't seem interested.

"Perhaps you're right," continued Fred, puckering his face and pretending to hold his nose, "I can still remember the awful smell when I buried my head in his fat belly to free him from the window. I don't fancy having to do that again. Come on, let's get out of here."

The dog turned its head, looked up at Fred, and gave a short, sharp bark and, whether it was in agreement or not, like long-lost buddies, the two of them set off up the lane in the direction of the town.

Once he felt sure he was out of sight of the house, Fred sat down on a grassy bank at the side of the road. His newfound friend trotted over to join him.

"Now tell me," said Fred as he absent-mindedly pushed his hand into the dirty, tangled hair of where he thought the dog's neck might be—for it wasn't immediately obvious which end of the shaggy mat in front of him the dog kept its head—"where do you live?"

Realising it was a bit of a daft question to be asking a dog, he asked another equally daft question.

"Do you have an owner?" and paused as if expecting the dog to answer.

"Let's see if you have a collar with your owner's name and address on it," and he rummaged around in the dog's hair looking for something which might give him a clue.

Unable to find one, Fred gave up looking and continued his chatter.

"If you don't mind my saying so, you look as if you're wearing an old rug someone chucked in a dirty dustbin!"

He thought about what he'd just said and, wishing he'd not said it, for it was rude, he changed the subject.

"Tell me," he said, trying to think of what to say next, "with all that hair in front of your eyes, how do you see where you're going? I've often wondered how Old English Sheepdogs find their way around."

He paused, as if waiting for an answer, and then ploughed on.

"Do you wear night-time goggles?"

Now Fred was on a roll, there was no stopping him.

"Do you use radar?"

"Do you have a foldaway white stick with a rubber bit on the end of it?" and running out of stupid questions to ask, he stopped and asked the most obvious one:

"Have you got eyes?"

Fred made an educated guess that the dog's eyes were halfway between the two lumps on the side of the end facing

46

him and the pink bit that was sticking out, hanging down and covered in slaver. Taking aim, he reached forward somewhere between them and lifted up the tangled mass of hair that was dangling down. Two soft, milky-blue, round eyes stared out at him.

I have no eyes that you can see, they hide behind my hair
But see I do, as I can prove, for you are over there.
It's dark in here but I can see, as long as my hair joggles.
Day or night, dark or bright, for I wear night-time goggles.

Fred said the poem out loud as he was making it up, whilst the dog, with its head leaning slightly to one side, looked up at him wondering if he'd lost his senses.

"Are you alone in the world, old boy?" asked Fred when he stopped giggling at the nonsense of his poem. "What do you say we team up? ...become buddies? ...hang around together?"

He paused between each question, hoping the dog would say something, hoping it would agree.

"You poor old thing," he said, dropping the carpet of hair back over the dog's eyes and forcing his fingers through the tangle of hair on the dog's back.

"You need a good bath," he said. "And so do I, if the truth is known… But I don't see how I'll get one at Uncle Victor and Aunty Nora's. They don't seem to have a bath."

The dog flopped its head onto Fred's lap and let out a sound that Fred mistook for a sigh. And they sat together like this for some time, as if lost in their thoughts.

"If you don't have a dog collar," mused Fred, breaking the silence, "I'm guessing you don't have an owner? And if you don't have an owner, you probably don't have a name either?"

By now, Fred had worked out he was talking to himself, for the only reaction the dog made to his questioning was to turn its head onto the other side and drop a large, slimy, glistening blob of saliva onto Fred's lap.

"Why don't I give you a name then?" he said, suddenly excited. "Mind you, I'm pretty naff at making up names—not like Dad, he was great at it—but it might be fun to try."

In the next few minutes, he rattled off numerous dog-sounding names as they came into his head, but none seemed to fit.

"I told you I was no good at it," and thinking of nothing better to do, Fred sang his Chocolate Robin poem.

> *"When you're feeling sad or gay*
> *Turn around, and smile and say*
> *Chocolate Robin!"*

"That's it!" he cried, leaping to his feet and startling the dog.

"Oh, I'm sorry. I didn't mean to wake you up, it's just I've thought of a great name for you. It's unbelievable how stupid I can be at times! Why didn't I think of it before? With that big, brown splodge of colour in the middle of your chest, I've got the perfect name for you. We'll call you Chocolate Robin."

And without waiting for the agreement that he knew he wouldn't get, he grabbed the dog by its front paws and danced it around in a sort of circle whilst he sang the Chocolate Robin song over and over again.

"Now, what do you say we get something to eat? I'm starving!"

Chapter 7
The Butcher

"Can you smell that, Chocolate Robin?" said Fred long before the fast food shop came into sight.

"Cheeseburger and French fries, here I come."

He thrust his hand into his pocket for his money and then remembered he'd hidden it in his sock for safety. He walked the short distance back to the public toilets they'd passed on the way into town, went into a cubicle, and took off his shoe. There were four 20-pound notes and two 10s stuffed inside his sock.

He unfolded the small bundle, took out one of the 10s, slid the remaining notes back inside his sock, and refastened his shoe.

The hamburger was greasy; just the way he liked it.

"By golly I needed that," he said when he finished scoffing it down. "Now, let's see if we can get something equally revolting for you."

Throughout the meal, Chocolate Robin had sat with his tongue hanging out watching Fred eat. Small drips of saliva accumulated on the dog's tongue, ran down the tip, hung there suspended for a moment, and dripped onto the ground. Drop by drop, a small, sticky puddle formed between the dog's paws.

With the back of his hand, Fred wiped the gunge and tomato ketchup off his face and got to his feet. He put the hamburger wrapper in the litter bin.

"Come on, old mate, now it's your turn."

Hearing these words, the dog jumped to its feet and hurried off across the open piece of land in front of where they were sitting. Hoping the dog knew where it was going, Fred followed, but even at a walking pace Chocolate Robin went too fast for Fred to keep up without running, and, by the time the dog arrived at the place it had chosen, Fred was way behind.

"You're not as stupid as you look," said Fred when he saw they had come to a local butcher's shop.

"I'm sorry, but dogs are not allowed in. I'm afraid you'll have to stay outside, boy... Unless you are a girl, that is?"

The dog didn't seem bothered one way or the other, or if it did, it didn't say so.

"Do you have any old bones?" asked Fred when it was his turn at the counter.

"The cheek of kids today!" barked the young man who was serving as he took a step back from the counter and stood up to his full height so everyone could see how superior he was. "What do you think this is... a charity shop? We sell meat here, we don't give it away!"

The assistant peered over the counter and looked down his nose at Fred as if he was little more than a dirty piece of paper he'd used to wipe poo off his shoe. "Now get lost, and take your scruffy dog with you,"

The young man turned towards the lady whose turn it was in the queue and gave her a smug, 'aren't I clever?' smile. "Sorry about that, madam. We have to put up with riff-raff like that every day."

The way the man answered Fred's simple request was one of the things Fred had never understood about grown-ups. He tried to rationalise it. Perhaps the man had thought Fred wasn't going to buy the bones. But even if he had, he didn't have to be rude. Why do so many adults think the worst of children and not the best? Why is it that when people get older many of them lose their sense of humour? It is as if people are born with a bag full of 'fun and nonsense' and that, as time goes on, a hole wears in the bag and the silliness inside falls out and runs away like water from a tap.

Fred went outside the shop and tried to explain to Chocolate Robin what had happened and why he had come out empty handed. The dog looked up at him as if listening. If Fred hadn't known better, he would have sworn he saw the dog shrug its shoulders.

"Don't worry, boy, we'll find a supermarket and buy some meat there… But it won't taste as nice. For one thing, they don't sell meat with the bones on… And for another, you have to pay more than at a proper butcher."

He heard himself add the bit about money, even though he knew it was a silly thing to say to a dog, but having some money gave him a feeling of security; the only money he had in the world was what he'd stuffed in his sock, and he knew it wouldn't last long.

As Fred was talking away to Chocolate Robin, a rotund man with a cheery face came out of the butcher's shop. He hesitated and gave them a smile as if he'd seen them before. The man's clothes were clean and tidy but otherwise unremarkable. In fact, everything about the man was so unremarkable Fred hardly noticed him.

"I hope you don't mind my asking, but is that your dog?"

"Sort of," said Fred.

"And what kind of sort of is sort of?" the man's eyes sparkled as he asked the question.

"It's hard to explain, sir, for I only came here today."

Chocolate Robin must have decided he liked the man, for he went towards him wagging his tail.

"I saw the dog wandering in the lane this morning and we've sort of teamed up," added Fred.

The man bent down and stroked Chocolate Robin. A fine plume of dust puffed up from the shaggy hair on the dog's back and settled on the man's hand. Noticing it, the man thought about wiping it off on the plastic bag he was carrying but, out of politeness, decided not to.

"Ah! That sort of sort of."

The man turned and ambled off towards the alley at the side of the shop. He lifted the lid of a wheelie bin standing there and dropped the plastic bag into it. He closed the lid and came back over.

"Here," he said, "I brought this for your dog."

And, like a magician producing a rabbit from a hat, he reached into the pocket of his jacket and pulled out another plastic bag.

"Be discrete and don't let my son see you open it."

Fred took the bag and, guessing the son the man was talking about was the shop assistant who'd refused to serve him, he turned his back on the shop window and peeked into the open neck of the bag. Inside were several bones covered with meat.

"Are these for me?" asked Fred.

"No," said the man. "They're for your dog." And they both smiled.

"Thanks," said Fred. He paused for a moment, not knowing what to say next.

"If you don't mind my asking, are you the owner of the shop?"

"Indeed I am. How clever of you to work that out, given that I'm not dressed like a butcher. I've been down to the cattle market this morning; it's nice to wear ordinary clothes sometimes.

You probably didn't notice me when you came into the shop; I was sitting in the back having a cup of tea. I must apologise for my son's rudeness. No matter what I say to him, he doesn't seem to understand the meaning of good manners."

"That's alright," said Fred. "I understand. But you've no need to apologise to me. My dad always told me you can never apologise for other people's behaviour; you can only be responsible for your own."

Fred put his hand into his pocket and took out the money he'd been given as change at the fast food shop. "How much do we owe you?"

"Let's call it nothing," said the butcher.

A look of surprise, followed by one of disbelief, spread across Fred's face.

"That's very kind of you," he said, somewhat shocked. "Then nothing it shall be!"

To make what he said sound funny, he imitated the voice of a character from a Charles Dickens story he'd seen on the television. Then he had an idea. He took the money he had in his hand and transferred them, one coin at a time, from one hand to the other. When he'd finished, he hunched his shoulders and slipped the coins into his other pocket in a way he thought a miser like Ebenezer Scrooge might have done. Then, with the flourish of a magician, he thrust a hand into his empty pocket, rummaged around, and pretended to pull out a large handful of imaginary money he'd found there.

"Here you are, kind sir," he said.

One at a time, he placed the imaginary notes of money into the palm of the butcher's outstretched hand and, speaking in the manner of people who lived at the time of Charles Dickens, said, "I insist you take this as recompense for your troubles. Pray keep it as a token of our thanks!"

"That's very kind of you."

Playing along with the game, the butcher made a small informal bow and touched his forelock and continued, "And I hope we shall continue to have the pleasure of your custom at our humble establishment."

"I sincerely hope we shall," said Fred, enjoying himself immensely as they mimicked the manners and language of the 19th century. "May I take this opportunity to bid you a good day, Mr. Marlow, and a woof from my faithful friend here at my side?"

The butcher looked surprised that Fred knew his name, then smiled as he guessed he'd worked it out from the sign above the shop, 'Marlow and Son, Butchers'.

"And what, pray, is your name, young man?"

"Fred it is, sir, Fred Smith; and this… this is my sort of dog! His name is Chocolate Robin, but I regret he hasn't, as yet, learned to say it."

With this final exchange they parted company and understood, without needing to say it, that they would meet again.

Mr. Marlow turned and went into his shop. Fred and his four-legged friend set off to the nearby park. And whilst Chocolate Robin got down to the serious task of devouring his bones, Fred got down to telling him how, one day, they'd have lots of money.

Chapter 8
Sheep

Feeling fully fed, the two friends set off for home. They stopped at a small grocer's on their way and bought chocolate powder, flour, butter, and a couple of boxes of eggs. Hoping not to be noticed, Fred popped in at a chemist's and bought some powdered milk for babies.

The leafy country lane leading down to Appletree Cottage was bordered by a wood on the left and a series of open fields with sheep in them on the right. In contrast to the sheep, pristine and white in their new coats, Chocolate Robin looked more scruffy and dishevelled than ever.

"Do you know how the sheep keep so white?" asked Fred, who couldn't help but notice the difference between them and his newfound friend, and, without waiting for a reply, or indeed thinking about his friend's feelings, he answered his own question. "They use the sheep dip every day!"

Chocolate Robin showed no interest in Fred's half-hearted attempt at a joke and sauntered on in front as if nothing had been said.

"Tell me something. I can see you're a Sheepdog. When you look at all those sheep wandering about all over the field, does it not make you want to go in there and tidy them up?"

Fred stopped walking and turned towards the impressive five-barred gate guarding the entrance to a field.

"You know, I feel sorry for sheep. I mean, it's not fair if you think about it. I've just had a huge meal of hamburger and chips, not to mention a big dollop of ketchup. And you,

you've just stuffed down a load of juicy bones. But all sheep get to eat is grass. And short grass at that," he added as an afterthought.

"What do you say we go in there, round up the skinniest of the sheep, and give them a real feast?"

Chocolate Robin, who by now was some distance off in the lead, stopped in his tracks and turned to look at Fred.

"There's not much for them to eat here and I know where there's a whole load of really long, juicy grass just waiting to be gobbled up."

Fred had hardly finished talking when Chocolate Robin gave a short bark and rushed off towards the field. Reaching the gate, he took a couple of short bounds, jumped up onto the top bar, and hopped down onto the grass on the other side. He landed with an almighty thud.

"Attaboy," said Fred, who took up position standing on the bottom bar of the gate. He leaned over to watch what the dog was up to.

"Don't get carried away in there," he shouted. "We can't take them all; Uncle Victor's front garden's not big enough for them all."

By now, Chocolate Robin had reached the far end of the field, so it was doubtful if he heard what Fred had shouted and, even if he did, that he would have understood. He was, as Fred was finding out, just a Sheepdog, and he was doing what Sheepdogs do best.

Hugging the hedge that surrounded the field, and apparently ignoring the sheep, Chocolate Robin set off around the edge of the field as if out on an afternoon stroll-to relax and enjoy the morning air.

The truth was that this was far from the case. In no time at all, and without any fuss or bother, he'd singled out from the flock twenty or so of the skinniest looking sheep and was shepherding them down the field towards the gate.

Fred was so busy admiring how easily his friend had chosen and rounded up the sheep that he forgot he would have to open the gate to let them out. Indeed it wasn't until the sheep started bumping against the gate and he heard Chocolate Robin bark that he even thought about it.

"Sorry, old boy, I was miles away… Admiring a professional at work."

Fred jumped down off the bottom bar and opened the latch holding the gate. He then put one foot back on the bar and, like a skateboarder at the beginning of a race, pushed off as hard as he could with his other foot. Unfortunately, the gate opened more quickly than he anticipated.

Being a big gate, it swung round in the large arc of a circle that took it at an ever-increasing speed out towards the lane before finally swinging back towards the field. Having nothing to stop its motion, it came to a sudden halt when it slammed into the hedge and embedded itself there.

"Yippee!" shouted Fred as the impact shook his bones up, almost throwing him off. He was thinking of doing it again when Chocolate Robin let out a sharp bark as if to tell him to stop messing about, for there was work to do.

Worried the sheep might rush off up the lane towards the town, Fred jumped down off the gate to cut off their path. Frantically waving his arms in the air, he made as much noise as he could to frighten them. But he needn't have bothered, for the sheep showed no interest. It was as if they had been pre-programmed and knew where they were going, for they all dutifully turned to the right and set off down the lane in the direction of Appletree Cottage.

"Now for the tricky bit," said Fred when Chocolate Robin and the twenty or so sheep had left the field, "pulling the gate out of the hedge and shutting it before the rest of the flock make a run for it!"

The gate was so firmly stuck in the hedge it proved difficult to free it. A few well-aimed blows of his boot, however, did the trick and Fred managed to shut it again before any of the other sheep could escape from the field.

He set off after Chocolate Robin and the sheep and when he caught up, he began poking fun at his friend.

"It's so easy to round up sheep, Chocolate Robin. I can't see what's difficult about being a Sheepdog! Nothing to it!

All you have to do is walk behind them; being sheep, they do all the rest. You don't even have to waste energy giving them a good woof!"

If Fred was trying to wind up Chocolate Robin, it didn't work. As usual, his friend ignored him and carried on sauntering behind the flock that, for all the world, seemed to be finding their way as if on autopilot.

"Ah!" shouted Fred so loudly that the sheep at the back of the flock turn around in surprise. "You're going to need my help getting them through the gate of the cottage and into the front garden. Tell you what, I'll push on ahead and open the garden gate and stand in the road and shoo them. Don't worry, old boy, I'll take care of everything."

To get in the front, Fred tried to force his way through the flock. The sheep wouldn't have anything of it. Whenever he tried to squeeze through a gap in their numbers, it was as if they knew what he was going to do and closed it up again to block his path. After several fruitless attempts, he gave up and cut off into the wood to get past them that way.

What seemed an obvious solution to his problem was not as easy as he first thought for the undergrowth in the wood was so thick he had difficulty walking through it, never mind running. There were hidden rocks everywhere and he had to be careful of tripping over them. He also had to be careful of sinking his foot into the numerous rabbit holes hidden in the ground and of twisting his ankle.

A barn owl sitting high up on a branch of a tree saw Fred come into the woods; its beady black eyes dotted against its heart-shaped white face gave it a surreal appearance as it stared down at him.

Although Fred hadn't seen the owl, a prickly feeling in the hairs at the back of his neck gave him the feeling he was being watched. He stopped and looked around. He saw nothing at first, then chanced to glance up.

High above, peering down at him like a judge waiting to pass sentence, the owl sat impassively on its branch. It closed both eyes, opened them again, then let out a gentle 'scree' sounding noise that slipped out of its beak and reverberated through the woods.

"And the same to you," said Fred, "and whilst we're at it, don't just sit there staring at me, there's work to be done? I could do with your wings!"

Like Chocolate Robin before him, the barn owl was totally uninterested in what Fred was saying and sat there watching him as he set off again in his effort to overtake the flock.

An animal track through the undergrowth in the wood made Fred's going easier and, by the time he left the woods and reached the cottage, he had a good lead on the sheep. He ran over to the garden gate tangled in the hedge and bent down to yank it free with both hands. He paid the price. Not happy with being disturbed, the brambles holding the gate sunk their barbs into him, drawing blood.

"Right!" shouted Fred licking his wounds, "you asked for it," and lunging at the hedge, he laid his trusty boot into their thorny tangle. After two or three good kicks, the brambles cried out for mercy and fell back in retreat, taking the gate with them!

"Oh, dear, what a clever clogs you are, Fred Smith! You've made plenty of room for the sheep to get in, but now there's no gate, you've also made plenty of room for them to get out again!"

As he stood contemplating what to do next, a tiny current of air brushed his cheek and a flash of white caught his eye. The barn owl had come to join him. Landing noiselessly on a tree stump sticking up out of the hedge a few feet from where Fred was standing, it settled itself down as if to watch the fun.

"What's this, a front row seat, or an offer to help?"

The owl closed both of its eyes and opened them again.

"Well, if you're going to hang around, how about you guard the gate for a week or so and keep the sheep in? What do you say?"

The owl had nothing to say.

The first of the sheep to arrive hesitated when it saw Fred standing in the middle of the road waving about like an over-wound clockwork traffic warden.

"In there," he said nodding his head and pointing it in the direction of the gaping hole he'd made in the hedge. "And once you're in, you have to stay in and follow the rules! In return for good food, you have to follow the first rule, it's called the 'no escape 'til I say so' rule."

The lead sheep raised its head, let out a 'baa', and ambled off through the gap and into the garden.

"I'll take that as a 'yes' then," said Fred.

One by one, the rest of the sheep followed the first into the garden and settled down to munch the grass.

"You stay there, Chocolate Robin, and keep them in and I'll get some branches from the wood to block up the hole. Uncle Victor will be thrilled when he sees what we've done."

"NORA! NORA! What are all those sheep doing in the front garden?"

Uncle Victor's enormous frame appeared at the window. Unfastening the latch, he pushed the window open and leaned out. "SHOO! SHOO! GET AWAY. YOU'RE NOT WANTED HERE!"

"Oh, no," said Fred from the safety of the woods. "He's going to get stuck in the window again."

Chapter 9
Sweets

One at a time, Fred dragged a load of dead branches across the road from the wood to block up the hole in the garden hedge where the gate had once stood. Satisfied the sheep were properly penned in, he went around the back of the house to look for the ladder to climb into the house through the attic window. Having nothing better to do, Chocolate Robin tagged along behind him.

Hidden from view behind the house, Fred found a garden shed and, buried in the long grass behind the shed, a ladder. Out of curiosity, he pushed the door of the shed open and looked inside.

"It's nice and dry in here, Chocolate Robin. I don't know where you plan to sleep tonight, but you could do worse than try in here," he said, hoping the dog would take up the offer.

Untangling the ladder from the clutches of the undergrowth proved almost as difficult as the efforts with the garden gate, but, once it was free, it proved easy enough to lift and carry, for it was made of light aluminium. Fred set the feet of the ladder in the grass immediately below the window of the attic and, quietly, so as not to disturb Uncle Victor, leaned the main body of it up against the roof.

"Ah!" he exclaimed when he saw the drainpipe he'd broken off as he'd slid down the roof. "I'd forgotten about that."

He took a step back to look at the damage and see what could be done about it.

"Chocolate Robin, I don't know about you, but I'm not very good at mending things? I don't think it's snapped, I think I've just dislodged one of the connecting pieces," he added, half to encourage himself and half in the hope that his friend, who'd decided to sit down next to him, might come up with a brilliant idea.

He turned and looked at the dog.

"What do you think, old boy?"

Chocolate Robin stretched himself out on the grass to enjoy the sunshine and showed no interest. Undeterred, Fred carried on talking.

"If I can push the drainpipe up and position it next to the hole in the gutter it came out of, all I'll have to do is to give it a good push and it will just snap back into place."

He tried to sound positive about the idea, but it was obvious from his voice that he was not at all sure, either that he would be strong enough to do what he wanted to do, or that it would work. But, having no better plan, he took the pipe in both hands and lifted it up until it was almost in line with the hole.

"Here we go, old boy. Wish me luck."

Fred gave the drainpipe one almighty push and, hey presto, it snapped back into place.

"Well, that was easy; must be my birthday!"

If Fred's arms had been long enough, he would have patted himself on the back, but, as his dad hadn't been an orangutan, he gave Chocolate Robin a pat instead.

"Here's hoping my cooking goes just as well."

Fred sat down on the grass, wrapped his arms around Chocolate Robin, and gave him a cuddle. He was about to tell him how much he'd enjoyed their day together and how he was looking forward to many more when the dog turned and gave him a great, big, slobbering lick on his face.

"Thanks, that'll save me from having to wash tonight."

The two friends sat together for some time before Fred decided it was time to get up. He put his foot on the bottom rung of the ladder.

"I have to leave you now and start the cooking," he said and, in spite of the fact he knew he was only really talking to himself, he chose his next words carefully.

"I'll see you in the morning then?"

He phrased it like a question. He thought of saying, 'I hope I'll see you in the morning', but that meant there was a possibility the dog wouldn't be there. 'See you in the morning,' sounded more positive. As did 'Of course I'll see you in the morning, because you'll be there,' but that wouldn't have been polite. He settled on 'I'll see you in the morning,' and stuck a 'then' at the end to make it sound like a question and to give it what he hoped would be a friendly touch.

Deep down, Fred didn't want to go back up to his room in the attic.

"Tomorrow is my first day at my new school," he continued, to keep the conversation going. "I had a difficult time starting in my previous school. It was the middle of term—as it will be tomorrow at my new school. All the kids knew each other. By then, they all had their friends and I was Mr. Stranger stuck on the outside looking in."

To stop himself from thinking miserable thoughts, Fred clicked his fingers. At times like this, he would usually sing his Chocolate Robin song, but, right now, for some reason, he didn't feel like it.

He busied himself adjusting the ladder, pulled its feet back a little, and then a little more. Finally, after a bit of wiggling, it rested flat along the slope of the roof of the house. Satisfied he'd got it right, he turned towards the dog.

'Bye then,' he said and climbed up and through the open window into the attic before looking back. Almost hidden in the long grass, he could see the sheep were chomping away.

"Take care the tigers don't come and chomp on you," he called.

The barn owl, still ensconced on the tree stump, looked up at him, closed both its eyes, and opened them again.

"And a good night to you, Owlie! See you in the morning too." He lengthened the 'too' at the end into a 'too-wit-te-woo' and smiled. The owl didn't seem impressed.

Once inside, it took a few moments for Fred's eyes to adjust to the gloom of the attic. Remembering he'd left the candle and box of matches close to the window, he groped around in the layers of muck and filth on the windowsill until he found them.

He took out a match, lit the candle, and looked at the wiggling trails his fingers had left in the dirt. *Looks like snakes live here as well as tigers,* he thought.

He made a mental note to clean the place one day and then had second thoughts. Knowing that tomorrow never comes, he promised himself he would do it tomorrow and set off across the attic to go down to the kitchen to start the cooking. So as not to disturb the slumbering walrus in the front room, he made as little noise as possible climbing down the ladder.

Inside the kitchen, he had to rummage around to find a bowl big enough to put the dozen eggs into. There was only one bowl. It was much too small, so he carefully placed the eggs, one at a time, onto the counter and hoped none would roll off and fall onto the floor.

He measured some of the ingredients he'd bought on their way home into a saucepan, mixed them together, and cooked them carefully. Whilst the mixture was still moist, he plopped dollops of it into the hollows in the egg boxes the eggs had been in.

Using a fork, he mounded the dollops into cone shapes and made swirl marks that spiralled up their sides like a series of parallel footpaths on a mountain. He finished his decoration with a sprinkling of chocolate powder; Fred's ideal vision of snow: the chocolate sort!

Aunty Nora must have heard a noise in the kitchen, and came to see what was happening. Closing the living room door gently behind her, she swooped up behind Fred with the silence of an owl. He felt a warm draft of air brush past his face and thought for a moment Owlie had come to join him.

"I've made a few sweets to take to school tomorrow," said Fred when he realised it was his aunt and not the bird. And, feeling he had to explain what he was doing in her kitchen without having asked, he said rather lamely, "I didn't want to disturb Uncle Victor."

He stopped what he was doing and turned to face her. "I hope that was alright."

Fred could tell from the look on Aunty Nora's face that she hadn't been listening. Her eyes were focused on the sweets he'd made, her mouth open in surprise.

"They look so nice," she said.

"Would you like to try one?"

"Yes, please," she replied, "but don't you think you should keep them for you."

"Thank you," said Fred. "I've made them for school tomorrow, but I'm not sure I'll have enough. I should have bought more ingredients."

He left it at that. He could have gone on to explain his thinking, but decided against it and tidied away his things instead.

"See you at breakfast," he said and climbed back up the ladder into the attic.

"7 o'clock," said his aunt. "School starts at 9."

Chapter 10
Unwelcome Visitors

Before Fred could lie down to sleep on his mattress, he had to fill it with air. It proved to be more difficult than he thought, for, after every minute of blowing into the nozzle, white dots appeared in front of his eyes and he felt dizzy. It took at least fifteen minutes before there was enough air in the mattress for him to use it as his bed.

He picked up the two blankets his aunt had given him to keep warm during the night, but they were so thin he could easily see the light of the candle through them. Rather than be cold, he decided to sleep with his clothes on.

He put his suitcase down at the foot of the mattress, picked up his two egg boxes of sweets, and stacked them one on top of the other. It took him all of two seconds.

With the whole evening in front of him, Fred mulled over what to do with the rest of the time before going to bed. His first thought was to get out a book and see if the candle would give out enough light to read by, but he remembered he had no book. To relieve his boredom, he played a game of trying to think up as many larlypoopycake ideas as he could, but the inspiration wasn't there. In fact, nothing was there, not even a chair to sit on.

He walked across to the window to see if anything was happening outside. Apart from the sheep playing hide and seek in the long grass, everything was quiet. Chocolate Robin and the owl were nowhere to be seen.

Fred thought of climbing back out of the window to go and look for them, but decided against it and walked back to his bed. Having nothing else to do, he turned and walked back to the window. He was a prisoner in a cage of cobwebs. Bored of pacing up and down the two or three steps from his mattress to the window, he lay down on his bed and tried to go to sleep.

He picked up the candle to blow it out and then changed his mind. If he woke in the night, it might cheer him up to see its light; if it hadn't burned itself out by then, of course. He made a mental note to buy a box of candles the following day; to give Chocolate Robin a big hug if he was still there in the morning; and wondered if the dog would sleep in the shed.

Getting to sleep wasn't easy. After a few minutes of tossing and turning on the inflatable mattress, Fred felt as seasick as the day he went on the ferry to France. Every time he turned over on his side the mattress moved with him and then pushed him back again. Backwards and forwards, backwards and forwards, it was as hopeless as trying to sleep on a rocking horse.

If he turned over too quickly, he was thrown off the mattress and onto the floor. Even if he tried turning slowly, he had to put his hand down onto the floor to stop himself from rolling off. There seemed no way he could win.

The bedclothes too had a mind of their own and refused to cover him all the time. He tried tucking them underneath the mattress, but they weren't wide enough. He tried tucking them underneath his body, but when he did he felt like an Egyptian mummy unable to move. Tired by his day, he eventually fell soundly asleep and it wasn't long before he was dreaming.

He was sitting at a small wooden table playing dominos with Chocolate Robin and the barn owl. Each time they finished a game, they'd turn the dominos face down and shuffle them. Moving them around and around on top of the table, they made a whirring, grating, gnawing sort of noise as they rubbed against the wood. Whirr, whirr… Pause, pause… Gnaw. Whirr, whirr… Pause, pause… Gnaw.

Fred opened his eyes with a start. The candle, although small by now, was still alight. The yellowy-white light from its flame spindled out across the room and was devoured by the cobwebs.

He saw two round, red points of light at the foot of the bed; then another two. They looked like cats eyes caught in the headlights of a car. Fred blinked. He was now looking at six points of light and not four. He stared at them. They stared back. He didn't move. They didn't move.

He tried to think what he could be looking at. He didn't recall there being anything at the foot of his mattress when he'd gone to bed. He could remember putting the suitcase there and stacking the two egg boxes of sweets on top to form a mini pyramid. But, apart from the spiders and their webs, the attic had been empty.

Fred sat up and a sudden scampering of tiny feet startled him. The points of light he'd seen only a moment before disappeared with them. He knew what they were. They were rats; enormous rats.

His first instinct, stupid though it was, was to chase after them, but, by the time he got to his feet, they'd scarpered and all he saw was a glimpse of their long, ringed tails as they scurried away into the shelter of the darkness.

But what was the gnawing he'd heard? Was it more than just a dream?

Still only half awake, it took him a few moments to realise what it was, the rats had been eating their way into the egg boxes to get at his sweets!

He reached down to see. The top box was untouched, but the bottom one had been gnawed through at one end. He opened it and looked inside. He was lucky. He'd woken early enough that they'd only had time to nibble the two sweets at that end of the box.

A shiver ran up his spine. He thought it was the cold causing it; then realised it wasn't. So why were his legs, his arms, and his body covered in goose bumps?

Fear!

Fear at the thought that he'd been sleeping on the floor with a colony of rats swarming all around him; his head lying only a few inches above the ground... At the perfect height for the rats to bite him. Had the sweets saved him? If they hadn't been there to attract them, would they have nibbled him instead?

There was no way Fred was going to try to go back to sleep. What was the point? How could he possibly shut his eyes without worrying they'd come back again. Checking his visitors had gone, he put on his shoes and went over to look out the window.

It was peaceful outside. Imitating a street light, the smiling face on the full moon illuminated the garden. Early signs of morning light were beginning to streak the sky. Morning was not far off. Below him, a few sheep were having their breakfast.

Fred looked for Chocolate Robin but couldn't see him. He hoped he'd taken his advice and slept in the comfort of the shed.

Having nothing better to do, he gazed out of his open window to wait for dawn. He listened to the town hall clock strike each quarter of an hour; counted the bongs at four, then five, and then six. At a quarter to seven, he picked up his precious egg boxes, slipped his toothbrush and toothpaste down the side of them, and, holding them in one hand, climbed down the ladder to get washed and ready for his first day at his new school.

Through the thinness of the door of the front room he heard Aunty Nora talking. She sounded agitated. Each time she said something, Uncle Victor's bullfrog of a voice batted it back against her. But she didn't give in. Each time he said no, she came back at him. He heard her take another tack, but his uncle countered that. She persisted. He persisted. Finally, their arguments died down. It was his aunt who had the last word. Had she won?

She opened the door. "Ah, Fred, I see you're down already. I was just about to call you. You'll be having breakfast in here with your uncle and me."

With his toothbrush in his mouth, Fred had an excuse not to answer. He finished cleaning his teeth, splashed a bit of water on his face and dried it. He left his toothbrush and toothpaste on the windowsill and, clutching his egg boxes under his arm, went into Uncle Victor's room.

"Good morning, uncle," he said in as cheerful a voice as he could muster.

"Good morning, Fred," replied Aunty Nora. "I trust you slept well?"

"Look at him," said Uncle Victor in his usual nasty way. "I told you he was stupid."

Fred opened his mouth. He was ready to answer back, to be nasty in return, but, like a glacier that stopped melting because it had run out of ice, his words evaporated into thin air.

"Victor! Remember what I just told you!"

From the way she spoke, it was obvious to Fred that the arguing he'd just heard had been about him. His aunt must have been reminding Uncle Victor that Fred was going to have breakfast with them and telling him to behave and be nice. Whatever it was she'd been saying, it worked, for Uncle Victor kept silent throughout the meal.

It didn't take long to eat breakfast; a slice of bread and margarine and a cup of tea. *Looks like I'll be eating out again*, thought Fred when he realised he was getting nothing else.

He asked his aunt to tell him how to get to his new school. It sounded easy and, if worst came to worst, he would follow the other children.

Before leaving, he opened the box the rats had eaten into and took out the two sweets they'd nibbled. He put them on the table in front of him and closed the box. He planned to throw them in a bin on his way to school. Or so he thought. The moment Fred lifted the lid of the egg box, Uncle Victor's eyes lit up. The sight of the chocolate swirls made his fingers start to twitch. A bead of saliva appeared at the corner of his mouth and, like a chameleon's tongue shooting out to grab its prey, he lunged forward to grab the sweets.

"More tea, Victor?" said Aunty Nora as she saw what was happening and grabbed hold of his shirt sleeve. She knew her husband well. It was all Fred could do not to smile.

"I'll be off now," he said, "I'll see you after school."

He turned, walked the few paces to the front door, said a quiet 'Hello again' to the coat stand as he passed, and lifted the latch. He braced his shoulder, pushed hard against door, and forced it open wide enough to squeeze out.

In his haste to leave, he forgot the two chocolate swirls he'd left on the table.

Uncle Victor didn't. He'd eaten them both before Fred left the house.

Chapter 11
School

The moment Fred saw Chocolate Robin waiting for him in the lane, all thoughts of his night-time encounter with the rats disappeared from his mind. He rushed over to greet him, gave him a big hug and bombarded him with questions. "Where did you sleep last night? Did you use the shed? Have you seen Owlie? Do you know the school I'm going to? Is it nice?"

As usual, Chocolate Robin didn't interrupt and let Fred ramble on without replying.

The walk to school took about twenty minutes. When they reached the school gate, they stopped and Fred explained to Chocolate Robin that dogs were not allowed inside.

"Off you go," he said. "I'll see you at home and I'll tell you about the rats I had to sleep with in the attic."

He gave Chocolate Robin a farewell pat and went inside the school yard. He called at the reception and asked which classroom he should go to. He was told to take a seat and that she would take him there after registration.

This was not what Fred wanted to hear. When he'd joined his last school, he'd been paraded into the class for all the students to gawp at. It wasn't a nice experience and for a long time, things had not gone well after that.

"Stand over there," said the teacher when Fred entered. She pointed to the corner of the room next to the window. One of the boys in the class called out, "Naughty boy, go and stand in the corner." Everyone laughed.

Fred did as he was told and pretended he hadn't heard the laughter. He stood next to the window and looked out. Ignoring what was going on around him, he waited for the teacher to ask him to come over to her desk.

"I didn't know you were coming today," she said as if it was Fred's fault. "I've no desk for you. You'll have to share mine for now."

"Teacher's pet! Teacher's pet!" came a cry from the back and the whole class picked up the chant. Everyone erupted into laughter again.

"Now let me see," said the teacher, ignoring the outburst. "You must be Smith. That's a simple name. I won't forget that in a hurry now, will I?"

"If he's got a simple name, Miss, does that mean he's simple?"

Fred knew it was best not to show his anger and waited for the teacher to tell the class to behave properly. But she ignored it.

In the short time Fred had been in the classroom, he'd noticed the teacher had already said 'now' on three occasions.

"How about we call him Smithy?" said the rather large boy who was the one who'd started the cry of teacher's pet.

"Simple Smithy," called out another, and smiled, obviously pleased with what he'd said.

"Or Sssssmithy the sssssimple," cried a third deliberately stuttering on the S's, pretending to have a speech impediment. Once more, the class erupted into laughter.

"Not so much noise now, children," shouted the teacher above the noise. "I have a few things to sort out now with Smith, before we start the lesson," she said throwing in a couple more 'nows'.

"Now let me see. Ah yes. I see you're down as having free school meals."

"Ain't he got any money, Miss?"

"He's not having mine," cried another.

"Or mine, Miss. My mam and dad go out to work so we don't have to sponge off others, Miss; not like Sssmiffeeeee?"

"Enough, children," shouted the teacher as she tried to stop the laughter before it got totally out of control. "Now take out your maths books."

Throughout the session until break time, Fred received taunts from various students. After the bell rang for break-time, he tried to hang around in the classroom until the others had left so he could be alone. However, several of the class had a different idea.

The noisiest of the groups of boys formed a ring around Fred, trapping him in the middle and they bundled him out into the playground.

"Where you from then?" asked the ginger-headed boy.

Not sure of how to answer, for whatever he said he knew someone would make fun of it, Fred took time to think.

"Don't talk much, does he?" said a rather scruffy boy who looked as if his house, like Aunty Nora's, didn't have a bath.

"The cat's got his tongue," said another and gave Fred such a hefty push, it knocked him to the ground. He instinctively thrust his hands out to protect his fall and in doing so dropped the boxes of sweets he was carrying. Luckily, they both landed upright, but their impact on the ground burst open their lids revealing the chocolate swirls he'd made the evening before.

"I'll have those," said the boy who Fred guessed was the leader of the bullies. He picked up both boxes and examined their contents.

"Right. Who wants to be first?"

"Me, Joe. Me," said one of the group as he leant forward and tried to grab one.

"Not so quick," said Joe, pulling the boxes close to his chest. "These little beauties look too good for you Bill. I think I'll keep them ALL for myself." He emphasised the 'all' rolling it out along his tongue like he was already enjoying the taste of the chocolate. The others knew he was teasing and groaned at him in much the same way as you do to the baddie in a pantomime.

"OK," said Joe. "Don't anyone say I'm not nice!" He paused and took a chocolate swirl out of the box. He examined it carefully, turning it around in his fingers as if he was handling a precious diamond.

"Pretty little thing," he said.

Joe brought the chocolate swirl up to his nose and gave it a sniff. He'd seen people do this with wine before tasting it and he thought it looked good. After a suitably long pause, he nibbled a bit out of it in much the same way as the rats must have done during the night.

"Not bad," he said. "Not bad at all."

He rolled his eyes, smiled and popped the rest of the swirl into his mouth in one go.

Deciding they'd waited long enough and it was their turn, the other boys pushed forward to grab a swirl before they were all gone.

"Where's your manners, boys?" said Joe, holding the box of sweets high above his head. He looked down at Fred who'd only just picked himself up off the ground.

"You don't mind if the others have one, do you, Sssmiffeeee?"

"Ssmiffeee says he'd love us to have one. Didn't you Ssmiffeee?" shouted one of the boys.

"You know what, Joneseee?" Joe elongated Burt's family name in the same way they had done with Fred's. He saw instantly that Burt didn't like it, so, like the bully he was, Joe teased him again.

"Joneseee's right boys. Smitheee says we can share the rest! But wait up… before you all go rushing and pushing and hurting yourself."

He slowly walked over to a small wall at the side of the playground and stood there for a moment as if waiting for a roll of drums.

"I'll just have another!" And with that, he popped a second chocolate swirl into his mouth and scurried off to let everyone fight over the rest.

Fred watched the expressions on their faces as they stuffed themselves with his chocolates. He could see how much they liked them and all the tension of a few moments earlier disappeared in an instant. For the rest of the morning, and even through lunch time, no one troubled him again.

Fred's problems, however, restarted in the afternoon. The class was down to play football and he didn't like football. He didn't like it for the very good reason that he was no good at it.

The games teacher that afternoon was the vicar. The vicar didn't teach at the school but he liked to help out from time to time and refereeing was one of the ways he did it.

The bullies chose the teams and were all on the same team. As Fred guessed, he was picked on the opposing team.

No sooner had the vicar blown the whistle to start the game, than the ball was kicked towards Fred. Like bees round a honeypot, in which Fred was the honeypot, the bullies all rushed after the ball. Pretending they were playing football, all they were really doing was kicking and pushing Fred.

To be fair, the vicar saw what was happening and did his best to stop it, but every time he took the ball away and restarted the game, the same thing happened.

Unseen at first, a dirty brown and white ball of hair on four legs burst onto the pitch and took control. Dribbling with its nose, it ran off with the ball towards the bullies' goal. It was Chocolate Robin, charging to Fred's rescue.

"Someone grab hold of the dog," shouted Joe, and they set off in pursuit of their prey.

Fred picked himself up off the grass and watched the fun as the dog ran in and out of the boys, teasing them with his ball control. Tiring of running round and round in rings, it set off again up the field with the ball, stopping now and again to let everyone catch up, but always keeping just out of reach.

Fred went closer to watch the fun.

Just in front of the goal area, Chocolate Robin ran so many rings around the goalkeeper that the boy gave up and fell down dizzy. With the goal at his mercy, Chocolate Robin put the ball down onto the penalty spot and waited.

Running faster than he'd ever run in his life, Fred was the first to react. Seeing the ball on the spot and no one in goal, he gave the ball a kick and scored the first goal in all his life.

The vicar blew his whistle awarding the goal and pointed to the centre circle.

The bullies were angry. They shouted that they'd been cheated. But no matter how much they shouted and argued that it wasn't a goal, the vicar refused to change his mind.

"That boys," he said, "could be called an 'Act of God'," and chuckled to himself.

"No, sir," said Fred. "You've misspelt the last word. It was an 'Act of Dog'!"

"Very good," said the vicar. "I like that!"

"And if you play around with the letters a bit more, sir, it makes 'Cat of Dog'."

And with that the vicar blew his whistle to end the game; Fred's team had won.

Chapter 12
Bedtime

When the bell sounded to signal the end of the school day, Fred hoped Chocolate Robin would be waiting for him outside the gates; but he was nowhere to be seen. Taking care to keep out of the sight of Joe and the other bullies, Fred hung around inside the school yard for a while. When he felt it was safe, he plucked up the courage to cross the road and hid behind some of the bushes. After half an hour, he knew Chocolate Robin wasn't coming, so he gave up and set off to buy the things he needed to do his next batch of cooking, calling in at the butcher's on the way.

"And a very good day to you, Mr. Marlow. I trust I find you well."

"I thought I told you not to come in here," barked the butcher's son before his father could answer.

"I made a little something for you," continued Fred, ignoring the son's rudeness, "but I regret to say it met with an unfortunate accident on the way here and I arrive empty handed."

That sounded nicer than saying the bullies at school had stolen the sweets and eaten them all.

"I shall endeavour to make amends this evening and rectify the position on my way to school tomorrow. Pray tell me at what hour you open."

"My good man," said Mr. Marlow using old English in the same playful manner as Fred had done. "I will open my establishment at six o'clock. I trust that will be in keeping with your requirements?"

The customers stopped what they were doing and listened in on their somewhat alien way of talking.

"Indeed it will, kind sir, but I regret I will be held up until a little nearer to eight."

"What are you two playing at?" said the butcher's son, raising his voice in frustration. "You're talking a load of rubbish!"

Fred looked at Mr. Marlow, who looked at Fred and then across to his son. He was enjoying the nonsense they were having but, at the same time, was not sure of how far he could push his son.

"I wonder if I might trouble you for a dozen and a half chipolata sausages… no make that a score if you would, for I'm forgetting that one of the recipients of the meal I'm concocting is… now how shall I put it… a little corpulent and wishes to keep it that way, if you take my meaning?"

"Indeed I do, sir. I take it the person to whom you refer is inclined to eat generously?"

"Quite, quite so," replied Fred. "Oh, and I almost forgot. A little something for my friend if you would be so kind," continued Fred who could see that the butcher's son was fuming as he watched his dad make a fool of himself.

"Pray, where is your friend?"

"I regret to say I cannot give you a satisfactory answer to that question."

Mr. Marlow's son was about to blow a fuse. His face reddened. He raised his fist and banged it down onto the work bench making his face go even redder. In an instant, more blood flowed into his cheeks than could be found on all the meat in the shop.

Fred decided the joke was over and that it was best to start speaking in normal English.

'Mr. Marlow, can I buy some empty egg boxes off you? I'll explain why I need them when I see you tomorrow."

The butcher counted out the chipolata sausages and wrapped them, but before giving them to Fred, he went into the back of the shop. He returned a moment later with a large stack of empty egg boxes and a plastic bag.

Fred handed him a five pound note, took back his change and popped it inside his pocket without checking it. With a "I'll see you at about eight tomorrow," he turned and sauntered out of the shop to buy the things he needed to make his sweets.

Later that evening when he emptied his pockets, he saw that Mr. Marlow had not charged him for his purchases. He'd simply taken the five pound note off Fred and given him five pounds in coins in return.

Walking down the lane towards Appletree Cottage, Fred was overjoyed to find Chocolate Robin waiting for him.

"I've got something for you," he said as he sat down on the grassy bank at the edge of the wood, facing the house. Inside the plastic bag, the butcher had given him, were several bones for the dog.

"By the way, thanks for what you did at school."

He looked at Chocolate Robin to see if he was listening, then continued, "It's strange when I think about what happened. It felt as if you knew what was going to happen and were waiting."

Sitting as they were, directly across the road from the cottage, Fred could see the sheep munching merrily away in the garden, and he noticed he'd left the attic window wide open. Luckily it hadn't rained.

'I'm hopeless at sporty things, Chocolate Robin, and yet today, at the end of the game, I seemed to be running faster than all the other boys, even the good footballers. And imagine… I scored the first goal in all my life."

He sat back and thought about what he'd just said. "I don't know old mate," he continued, "but since I met you, my life has become different somehow. Strange things seem to be happening that I can't explain."

Fred stopped talking and thought about what he'd just said. The last twenty four hours had been difficult at times. Two things in particular still troubled him. He didn't know which one was the worse: knowing he had to spend another night alone with the rats, or another day being bullied at school. In the end, he decided it was the rats for he knew he had to face them first.

"Chocolate Robin," he said, speaking out loud but really talking to himself, "I wish there were no rats in the attic. I don't know if you slept in the shed last night, but if you did, I've half a mind to sleep there with you."

The sight of the barn owl flying in low overhead caught Fred's eye. It landed on the chimney pot above the attic window. Given what had happened yesterday, there was nothing particularly strange about that. Nor when a few minutes later, two black cats sauntering down the lane appeared to look across at Chocolate Robin. Seeing he was busy munching on his bones, they wandered passed and into the front garden where they were quickly swallowed up by the long grass.

What happened next struck Fred as being much more unusual for two sparrow hawks swooped down and settled in a tree close to where he was sitting.

"Something's going on," said Fred. "I can feel it."

Chocolate Robin seemed too interested in his bones to have noticed.

The two black cats reappeared at the base of the ladder and, one behind the other, climbed up it and through the open attic window as if they lived there and it was something they did every day.

Outside in the lane and in the wood behind, everything had gone quiet. The arrival of the owl and the sparrow hawks had silenced any animal movements and, fearing for their safety, all the common birds had flown away.

The silence didn't last for long. A commotion broke out in the attic. A kafuffle was going on inside. A series of high pitched squeals of panic pierced the air as rat after rat appeared at the attic window and jumped out without looking. Sliding down tiles on the roof of the cottage, or launching themselves high into the air, they plunged down into the garden.

If they thought they'd made their escape they were mistaken; their problems had only just begun.

The barn owl and the sparrow hawks took up the chase. Dive-bombing from on high, they sunk their beaks and talons into the rats sending them scurrying down the lane faster even than Fred imagined he'd run that afternoon. From where he was seated, he had a perfect view of the action as rat after rat raced off down the lane as fast as it could go, not daring to look back.

"What do you think started all that Chocolate Robin?" he said turning towards his friend.

"Whatever it was," he continued when he saw he was going to get no reply, "the rats will be too scared to come back after that. I won't have to sleep in the shed tonight after all."

Chapter 13
Fred the Cook

"Hello," said Fred to Aunty Nora as he unpacked his purchases and put them down on the counter in the kitchen. "If it's all right with you, I thought I'd cook us all a meal tonight?"

From the look on his aunt's face, Fred couldn't tell if it would be all right or not. She stood there speechless with her mouth half open and a blank look in her eyes.

"I'm not bad at cooking," he continued, guessing his aunt would think he'd make a mess of it. "I bought some things I think Uncle Victor might like... and you too of course," he added when he saw her expression still hadn't changed.

There was a long moment of silence before Fred decided it was best to busy himself by finishing off the unpacking and give himself time to think of what to say next. He didn't fancy having to eat the twenty sausages all by himself for the rest of the week.

"I don't know if Uncle Victor would like that," she replied.

Fred's first thought was to say, 'I'll take that as a no then'.

"But it's sausages," he said trying to sound convincing. "I thought Uncle Victor would like sausages."

At the sound of the word 'sausages' two pictures sprang into Fred's mind: the first of his uncle; the second of a sausage. Separate objects initially, they began to merge until Fred pictured them standing next to each other. He had difficulty telling them apart. Both images were large. Both were round. And both were about to explode.

A smile drifted across his aunt's face. "Oh, Uncle Victor would like sausages!" And then, like a cloud passing in front of the sun, its light faded. "But do you not remember what Uncle Victor said when you arrived?"

Fred remembered many things Uncle Victor had said when he arrived, most of which he preferred not to. But yes, he knew what his aunt was trying to say but was afraid to put into words in case she upset him.

"I don't mean to come in and eat it with you," he said. "I'm quite happy to eat mine upstairs… or outside. It's quite nice outside. It's not raining."

Fred could feel his tongue tripping over his words. Why couldn't he just come out and say what he really felt. Of course, he didn't want to go upstairs and eat on his own. There was no table to eat on and no chair to sit on. And he wasn't in the mood for sitting outside on the grass, balancing a plate of sausage and mash. He wanted to eat a proper meal with a knife and fork, not have a picnic.

"That's nice of you, Fred." As his aunt spoke her shoulders relaxed and a sigh leaked from her mouth like air escaping from a small hole in a balloon. She'd already had one fight with her husband and won. That was more than enough for one day.

They agreed Fred would have the dinner ready for seven o'clock and that she'd come in and out of the kitchen and pretend she was doing the cooking. She wouldn't tell Uncle Victor that it was Fred. "No need to upset him."

She turned to go back into the front room and stopped. "Oh, by the way, Uncle Victor loved the sweets you left for him this morning."

"I'm glad," said Fred. "I'm going to make some more tonight. But they may not taste quite the same as yesterday's. The ones Uncle Victor enjoyed had a little extra something that came to me in the night and may never come back again."

It was obvious his aunt had no idea what Fred was talking about and, from where she was standing, she couldn't see his fingers crossed behind his back.

Fred made another twelve of the sweets he'd made the previous evening plus six each of four additional flavours: vanilla, which he crushed from the pod; peach and apple, which he made by squashing the fruit he'd bought; chocolate from melting a bar of chocolate; and marmite, which he got out of a pot. He had no idea if the people in this part of the country liked marmite, but it was very popular where he came from.

Thankfully, as he hoped, no rats came to visit him during the night and, although he woke from time to time to check, as I am sure you would have, he was so tired he got a good night's sleep.

Breakfast too was uneventful; either because his aunt had reminded Uncle Victor to behave or his uncle was on his best behaviour, hoping like a good boy, to be rewarded with a sweet. For fun, Fred decided to test to see if it was the latter.

He finished eating the slice of bread he'd been given for his breakfast and picked up his bag. He rummaged inside it as if looking for something. He took the opportunity to glance over at his uncle and saw his eyes light up. Without taking anything out, he closed his bag and set off for the door as if he were in a hurry to get to school. He'd gone no further than a couple of short steps before his uncle reached out his hand and held onto Fred's arm.

"Your aunty Vera was telling me you were busy cooking in the kitchen last night."

Fred saw the word 'sweets' pass across his uncle's eyes and down his nose. From there, they passed to the corner of his mouth where they hung upside down in the saliva that had begun to dribble down his chin.

"Oh, I almost forget," said Fred. "I knew there was something... Oh! It's just slipped out of my mind again. I must be getting old! Now what was it?"

Fred put his fingers against his chin and began stroking it gently. He pretended to be thinking, dragging out his uncle's agony for as long as he thought he could.

"Ah yes… I remember… I made these for you," he said, producing two sweets from out of his pocket like magic. "These two I made extra-large, Uncle, especially for you."

At the sight of the sweets in Fred's hand, his uncle's eyes began to stick out of their sockets like giant gobstoppers; at the smell of the chocolate, his nostrils began to flair; and at the sound of the cling film crinkling in Fred's hand, his ears began to twitch. It was not a pretty sight.

Fred leaned forward to hand the sweets across to his uncle and then paused.

"Perhaps Aunt Nora might like to share one?" he added out of devilment.

Quicker than the rats had disappeared down the lane, his uncle reached out and grabbed both sweets, and in no time at all, had unwrapped them and stuffed them into his mouth.

Outside, in the sunshine, the sheep too were stuffing their faces. Reaching the opening where the gate had once stood, Fred fought his way out through the barrier of branches he'd put there to block the hole.

Chocolate Robin was waiting for him in the lane.

"Busy day today, Old Boy," said Fred, giving him an affectionate pat and getting a wet lick in return. "Got to make a detour on the way to school. I have to see Mr. Marlow."

Fred accepted the grunt Mr. Marlow's son gave him as he entered the shop and returned it with a cheery good morning.

"Ah, Fred," said Mr. Marlow appearing from the room at the back.

"Good morning, Mr. Marlow," said Fred. "I've got something for you."

He took an egg box of sweets out of his bag and gave it to the butcher. "I'd like you to taste these for me if you would. They're a mixture of flavours. I'd like you to tell me what you think of them."

The butcher took the box and opened it. "Well, I'll tell you something straight away," he said, "they're a feast for the eyes. Well done. They make you want to try them. But if you don't mind, I won't taste them now for two reasons; I'm busy at the moment and it's too early in the morning for me to be eating sweets. If you come back after school, I'll let you know what I think then."

Mr. Marlow's son stopped what he was doing and craned his neck to see what was going on.

"I was hoping that one day, I could make money by selling them," said Fred, "but I'm not sure if anyone would want to buy them."

"I'd like to try them now," continued Mr. Marlow, "but as I said, I'm in the middle of doing something. Tell you what, I'll taste them in my tea break."

It was obvious that Fred wanted his answer immediately if not sooner but he knew it would be rude to ask Mr. Marlow to stop what he was doing just to taste them. There was nothing he could do but be patient and wait.

Chapter 14
The Second Day at School

As Fred thought it might, the bullying started even before he reached the school. A group of boys from a different class had heard about what had gone on the day before and wanted to join in the fun. It started when one of them shouted out, "Look there's Smiffeeee!"

Fred did his Chocolate Robin imitation and pretended not to have heard.

"It's Smifffeeeee, teacher's pet," called another.

"Bit of a dog at football," cried a third.

Hearing the word 'dog' he turned towards his friend but Chocolate Robin was no longer next to him. Fred looked around but couldn't see him. In a strange way, this pleased him. It was better the bullies didn't know they were together in case they started being nasty towards him as well.

Once inside the school gates, the bullies from his class came towards him. Caught as he was between the two groups, he felt helpless. It was then that an idea came to him. If he could play one group off against the other, it would give him a bit of a breathing space.

He remembered having the same problem at his previous school, and what he'd done then had given him the time he needed to become accepted; and the bullying eventually stopped. Perhaps it would work again?

Joe, the leader of the bullies in Fred's class, came over to him and as he did, so the bullies in the other group backed off.

Good, thought Fred, *that tells me Joe's group is the stronger.*

'Made any more sweets have you?'

"Don't you mean stolen them, Joe?" said Bill, thrusting his face forward.

"Yes I have," said Fred, 'but there's not time to get them out now, the bell's just gone. Tell you what, why don't I dish them out at break time?"

The expression 'saved by the bell' refers to boxing when one of the fighters is in trouble and the sound of the bell at the end of a round gives him a minute's break to recover. Fred felt he'd been 'saved by the bell'.

He'd tried to make his voice sound calm when he spoke, but deep down he was far from that. He wanted to give the impression they should trust him and be patient. He'd stood upright to his full height and noticed that he was probably the tallest of the group. But for whatever reason, what he'd said appeared to work, for everyone turned and filed into class without another word passing.

"I've got you a desk, Fred," said the teacher, calling him by his Christian name for the first time, "but I'm afraid there's no chair. You'll have to use mine for now."

"Teacher's pet, teacher's pet," shouted one the boys who was not a member of the gang of bullies but he quickly shut up when Joe turned round and said something to him.

Fred kept his head down throughout the morning and concentrated on the work set. But he wasn't doing his school work all the time; he was also busily preparing himself for what he'd planned next.

No sooner was he outside in the playground, than he was surrounded by Joe and his gang.

"OK, Smiffee," said Joe, shortening Fred's new-found nickname to just two e's. "Cough 'em up."

"OK," said Fred, "but stand back a little. Give me room to get them out of my bag. I don't want anyone knocking them over like one of you did yesterday."

The reference to what happened yesterday made everyone stand back and look around to see who it was who'd done the knocking over.

"That was Dave," said Bill. "He's daft like that."

"He'll not be daft like that again if he knows what's good for him," said Joe.

So far, Fred's plan was working. He'd drawn the attention away from himself and onto one of the others; in this case, Dave.

"I've made thirty sweets; six each of five different flavours."

Fred spoke slowly and deliberatively. He chose his words carefully. He hoped what he said didn't sound like he was giving a math lesson but he wanted to make sure the bullies knew he'd made them himself.

"I've cut the sweets into four pieces to give you a chance to taste each flavour."

Fred glanced up as he took the first box out of his bag; he wanted to judge their reaction. They were watching him intently; he could see he had their attention. So far it was going well.

"Joe," he said, turning to face the leader of the bullies, "why don't you give out the first lot?" He made a point of choosing Joe. Knowing that he was the leader, it was Fred's way of gently recognising the fact and of showing a little respect for his position.

He opened the egg box and passed it to Joe as if handling the crown jewels, and with a gentleness that surprised Fred, Joe took it from him.

"Now be careful because I've cut them into small pieces and they might be a bit crumbly. There should be enough for everyone. But try not to waste them. They're not easy to make."

Fred knew the bit about them being difficult to make was a slight 'porky' but he also knew it sounded good.

"Did you hear that, you lot?" said Joe. "Be careful when you take one… and make sure you only take one," he added.

Fred was more than delighted with how it was going. Without causing any offence to anyone, he was in control. It was going as well as he could ever have hoped. He could see that in the last few minutes, he'd earned a bit of their respect; if he was right. He hoped it would be the first step towards stopping them from bullying him.

"I like this one," shouted Dave. "It tastes like marmite and chocolate on toast. I'd never have thought of putting the two together. I'm going to try that on my toast tomorrow; Marmite and Neutella, me mam'll think I've gone mad!"

"What about this one?" said one of the others. "It tastes like chocolate, the really posh sort. I want another like that."

"The one I had," said Joe, "was like vanilla ice-cream, but I can't remember what the sweet looked like. Fred, can you help me?"

Fred was amazed. Since dishing out the sweets, not only had he not once been called Smiffee, or even Smith, but Joe had called him Fred; just as the teacher had done when he arrived in class.

"I'd love to help you, Joe, but I'm afraid between you, you've scoffed all thirty of them. Tell you what, would you like me to make some more for tomorrow?"

Fred didn't have to wait for an answer.

"But tell me," he said, "were there any you didn't like?"

"No," said everyone altogether.

"Then I'll make the same flavours as you had today and this time, I'll mark on the boxes which ones are which."

The rest of the day passed off without a problem and as soon as school finished, Fred set off to see Mr. Marlow. Chocolate Robin must have guessed for he was waiting for him outside the shop.

"Hello boy," said Fred, and gave him a big hug. "Where did you get to today? You were next to me on the way to school but when I turned around, you'd gone. It was probably just as well. I don't think it's a good idea the kids in school find out you're with me. It's bad enough if they pick on me. I wouldn't want them to pick on you as well."

He was so busy talking to Chocolate Robin, he didn't see Mr. Marlow come out of his shop to greet him.

"There you are, Fred," he said startling him by his sudden appearance. "Your dog looked tired sitting there waiting for you, so I gave him a little something to eat."

Fred was desperate to ask the butcher what he thought of the sweets but he didn't want to show it. All day, he'd been trying to choose what words to use but, now he was here, he couldn't remember what he'd planned and he ended up blurting out, "Did you have a nice day?"

"Yes, very, thank you."

"I mean…" said Fred, hesitating as his tongue tied itself into a knot.

Seeing the predicament Fred was getting himself into, the butcher helped him out. "If you've got a few minutes, I'd like to have a chat. Let's go over to the park and sit in the sunshine. There's so much I have to tell you."

Although the park was almost next to the butcher's shop, Fred couldn't believe how long it seemed to take to get there. His mind was racing. In making the sweets, he'd already spent over forty of the hundred pounds he had in his sock. If his sweets were not a success, he'd have wasted his money. What little he had left would soon run out. Then where would he be?

"Now Fred," said Mr. Marlow when they were seated on one of the old wooden park benches.

Fred looked up at the butcher's face and tried to read the expression on it. Had he liked the sweets, or was he going to say he liked them because that was the sort of thing adults often said to children? Was he even going to talk about them?

"I had a problem with the sweets you gave me."

Oh no, thought Fred. He reached out and wrapped his arms around Chocolate Robin's neck.

"A big problem," continued the butcher.

The blood drained from Fred's cheeks.

"This morning, I decided to cut each of your sweets into four pieces. I took one for myself and I gave one to my son.

I thought it best to let him eat his first. I'd love to have taken a picture of his face."

With fear dripping out of his eyes, Fred looked up at Mr. Marlow. "He didn't like it?"

"Didn't like it," replied Mr. Marlow, showing no emotion in his voice. "No, he didn't like it!"

Fred looked away and down at Chocolate Robin. He could feel the emotion building in his eyes.

"He didn't like it," repeated Mr. Marlow, "he loved it!"

At the sound of these words the pent-up tension drained out of Fred's body like a shiver running down his spine.

"He took another piece, then another, and then another," continued the butcher. "He loved them so much, I had to take them off him before he ate the lot. I put the rest on the counter far enough away so he couldn't get near them. But not before I tried my piece."

Fred didn't know what to say he was so excited.

"Each time a customer came into the shop, I offered them a piece. It was a difficult thing to do," he continued as if making an apology, "for if the truth is known, I wanted to keep them and eat them myself."

"But it would have been alright if you had," said Fred. "I gave them to you to eat."

"I know, but I wanted to see what other people thought of them."

"And..." said Fred unravelling his arms from around Chocolate Robin and sitting bolt upright as stiff as a soldier on parade. With every sense he could muster, he focussed all his attention on what the butcher was saying, listening for every word, every nuance he might make. It was as if his life depended on it.

"They loved them too!"

On hearing these few simple words, Fred's shoulders collapsed with relief and reflated just as quickly a moment later as the pride he felt flowing through him filled him with energy.

"In no time at all," continued Mr. Marlow, appearing not to have noticed Fred's strange behaviour in front of him, "word got around that we had some special sweets. A queue formed outside the shop. We had so many people wanting to try the sweets, we had to cut them into smaller and smaller pieces. In no time at all, they were all gone and we had to turn the people away."

Mr. Marlow was so excited telling his story, his mouth started dribbling. This caused Chocolate Robin's mouth to dribble too, although, if the truth be known, he was probably thinking more of juicy bones than Fred's sweets.

"Your sweets were good for our business. Everyone coming into the shop to taste the sweets felt they had to buy some meat. We sold more meat in one day than we do at Christmas."

"I'm pleased you did so well, Mr. Marlow," said Fred, pushing any thoughts of the success of his sweets out of his head and concentrating on his manners.

"Pleased Fred?" he replied. "We're delighted. My son thinks you're a genius."

And with that Mr. Marlow put his hand into his pocket.

"Here's twenty pounds. We want you to take it as a special thank you for all the business you generated for us today; and no arguing."

The expression on Fred's face as Mr. Marlow thrust the money into his hand was shock, coloured with disbelief.

"I'll make some more sweets, Mr. Marlow; but promise me you'll keep some for yourself; perhaps Mrs. Marlow would like to try them too?"

"I'd love you to do that Fred, but this time we'll buy them off you. We'd like to be your first customer, the first of many!"

"What do you mean Mr. Marlow, the first of many?"

"I think your sweets are so good, Fred, that you should seriously think of going into business and selling them to the general public."

Mr. Marlow's words flowed over Fred like an incoming Spring tide. They were everything he had wanted to hear… and more.

"But I wouldn't know how to go into business, and I'm not sure people would really be interested in buying them?"

"There's only one way to find out, Fred. Tomorrow is Saturday. It's market day. I have a stall at the market. Why don't you go straight home and make some sweets and bring them to the market tomorrow. Remember, it's the early bird that catches the first worm."

Chapter 15
The Market

Fred hid in the bushes, whilst he took a twenty pound note out of his sock. He folded it inside the twenty pounds Mr. Marlow had just given him, and with Chocolate Robin trotting along beside him, set off to the shops to buy all the things he needed for what he knew would be a long night of cooking.

"It's lamb chops for everyone tonight, Chocolate Robin. As well as giving me the money, Mr. Marlow gave me an extra present. There are more than enough chops for you too. What do you think of that?"

Chocolate Robin looked up—at least Fred imagined he looked up for the dirty bit of rug hanging from the front end of the dog moved and shook from side to side.

"Is that all you've got to say?" said Fred. "I would have expected at least a woof. It's not every day a dog gets to eat lamb chops. Come to think of it, are sheep dogs allowed to have lamb on their menu?"

Walking down the lane to Appletree Cottage, Fred saw the sheep milling about in the garden were making a good job of mowing the lawn. Soon it would be short enough to be able to cut with a mower.

'You know, Chocolate Robin, one day the farmer is going to find out part of his flock has gone missing. When he does, he's going to wonder how come they've all ended up in Uncle Victor's garden. Can you imagine the shouting there'll be if he knocks at the front door to get them back?"

As they were speaking, the barn owl flew across the road from the wood and settled itself on top of the chimney of the house.

"What do you say, when we've got some money we get a proper perch for Owlie," said Fred, "with a table, so he can have his meals in comfort?"

Chocolate Robin showed no interest in Owlie's comfort or eating habits. He was more bothered about when Fred would stop yacking and get down to dishing out the lamb chops.

"What do you think Owlie would prefer as a treat? Lamb chops, rat, or dinosaur?"

Chocolate Robin sat down and gave a double woof.

"Hungry, eh?" said Fred, picking up the message. "When I make some money selling the sweets, remind me and I'll use some of it to buy you a bowl to eat from."

"Woof," barked Chocolate Robin, which Fred took as agreement.

"Well, I can't hang around talking much longer. I've got cooking to do."

He took four of the lamb chops Mr. Marlow had given him and gave them to Chocolate Robin.

"Now eat up and don't forget the market will be an early start tomorrow. I've never done anything like this before. I hope you'll come with me to give me courage."

And with that, he climbed up the ladder and in through the window. Owlie sat watching from the chimney.

****

The instant Fred set foot in the kitchen, his uncle's fog horn sounded a new blast.

"What do you mean Fred cooked the meal last night! What do you think your job is?"

"But Victor…"

"Don't you 'but Victor' me. Keep him out of the kitchen. I'm not having him trying to poison me."

"But you enjoyed the meal last night, Victor. You said so…"

"That was before I knew he'd made it."

"And what do you mean by that?"

"What do I mean by that? I'll tell you what I mean by that."

But his uncle didn't know what he meant by that for his outburst was followed by a long pause.

"I'll tell you what I mean by that," he said, starting the fog horn up again. "I mean… I mean… he's not to go into the kitchen again."

Uncle Victor's words gushed out of his mouth like an old-fashioned railway engine letting off its excess steam.

"I forbid it. He can stay in his room upstairs. That's good enough for him," he added as if plopping a dollop of cream on top of a dessert for good measure.

Hearing his uncle's unpleasantness towards him, Fred couldn't control himself.

"Like it or lump it," he shouted, "I'm going to cook tonight's dinner. You can eat it or not, as you wish. It's your choice."

His sudden outburst came out of nowhere. Indeed, when he thought about it later, he had no idea why he said it, and he probably would have denied having said it if someone had asked him, for no sooner had he said it than he forgot what he'd said… if that makes sense.

Uncle Victor's response to Fred's outburst was dramatic and surprising. Instead of shouting back to tell him to behave himself—as he might have been expected to do—or to tell him he'd 'give him a thrashing'—as he'd so often threatened in the past—he said nothing; and a silence descended on the house like a blanket of snow. But the answer was quite simple. Until that moment, no one had ever shouted back at Uncle Victor. It took the wind out of his sails and becalmed him.

"It's lamb chops, tonight," shouted Fred who, now that he'd started, didn't seem to be able to stop. "And if you don't want them, I'll give them to the dog you haven't got!"

Hearing himself shout, it suddenly hit Fred how rude he was being, and he began to wish he hadn't. Being impolite was never a good thing, but he knew being rude was far worse.

"What I meant to say," said Fred, moving closer to the door so he didn't have to shout, "was that I am cooking lamb chops, green vegetables, and cauliflower, if anyone would like any. Shall I make it for 6.30 or 7?"

"6.30," came back Uncle Victor, almost before Fred had finished speaking.

****

With his sweet production in full swing, Fred hadn't time to sit down to eat his lamb chops, but then even if he'd wanted to, he couldn't have, for other than the spare chair in Uncle Victor's room, there was nothing for him to sit on.

It was nearly ten o'clock before he'd finished making the sweets. He was glad he'd taken far more egg boxes off Mr. Marlow that afternoon than he thought he would need.

By the time he'd washed up his dirty dishes and carried all the sweets upstairs, it was well past his bedtime. As he settled down to sleep, he worried if he'd wake up early enough to get to the market in time for the opening, without an alarm to help him.

As things turned out, he needn't have worried, for bright and early the following morning, he heard a tapping noise coming from the attic window. Thinking it was part of the dream he was having, he turned over and ignored it in the hope it would go away. But it didn't go away, and eventually, he dragged himself up out of bed to see what it was that was making it.

It was Owlie. Sitting on top of the open window, he'd been tapping on the pane with his beak.

"What's the matter, Owlie?" asked Fred. "We've eaten all the lamb chops if that's what you're after."

He heard the town clock strike six. "Thanks, old mate," he said, "but how did you know I had to get up early this morning? That's a mouse I owe you."

By the time Fred collected all his things together, he could see he had no time to get breakfast. He clambered out of the window and was delighted to find Chocolate Robin waiting for him in the lane.

Mr. Marlow was already at the market, by the time they arrived. He was busy setting out his meat on the large counter in front of him.

"Good morning, Fred. And good morning to you too, Chocolate Robin," he said turning to the dog. "I've put a bench at the end over there for you to arrange your sweets on. If anyone asks what you are doing selling them, tell them you're my nephew and you are just helping me out. You have to have a license to sell things; we'll use mine."

"Thanks, Mr. Marlow." Fred paused for a moment before continuing, 'Mr. Marlow, I've been wondering how much I should charge for the sweets? I've got no idea; I've never done it before."

"And nor have I, Fred. We'll just have to 'play it by ear' as they say… but don't ask me what ears have got to do with selling sweets," he added when he realised it was a funny expression to have used. "How about we start by charging 10p each?"

"And we could perhaps sell a box of six for 50p," said Fred, who'd already started working out how much money he'd make if he sold them all.

"Put out a plate with some free samples on; little piece that people can taste to see if they like them before they buy."

"Like you did in your shop," answered Fred.

"Yes, like in the shop."

When buying the ingredients the day before, Fred thought on to buy some nice pieces of card and some coloured pencils. He took them out of their bag, and in his best handwriting, set about writing out exotic names for the six different sorts of sweets he'd made. He then took two pieces of card and wrote in large letters the price of a sweet and the cost of a box of six.

All that now remained was to wait for the people to arrive.

This proved to be the hardest part.

Chapter 16
Success or Failure

The first person to show interest in Fred's sweets was a young boy.

"You must be joking," he said, poking his finger into one of the vanilla swirls.

"I beg your pardon," replied Fred.

"Look at that, Mam!" The boy grabbed hold of the sleeve of his mother's coat as she was trying to pay Mr. Marlow for the piece of beef she'd just bought.

"This idiot thinks people are going to pay 10p for one of them." He was about to poke his finger in one when Chocolate Robin, lying nearby, got to his feet.

Go get him, Chocolate Robin, thought Fred.

"We've no time for sweets now," said the mother. "We'll come when we've finished the shopping."

"Come back? I'm not coming back for them! I want some proper sweets!"

And with that, the obnoxious little boy leant forward to knock one of the boxes of sweets off the bench but changed his mind when he heard a deep throated growl behind him.

Mr. Marlow was doing a brisk trade selling his meat. As he chatted to the customers, he constantly took a few moments to tell them how delicious the sweets at the other end of the counter were. At that time in the morning, everyone seemed too busy to take him up on his offer. No one showed any interest.

Fred waited for Mr. Marlow to be free of customers and went over to talk to him.

"It's not working, Mr. Marlow. No one's interested in buying my sweets. I can't even get them to try them."

"It's early, Fred. People are not thinking about sweets; they've only just eaten their breakfast. The early morning shoppers are a different breed to those who come later in the day. Be patient, you'll see what I mean."

As he finished saying these words, a customer arrived. "Good morning, Mrs. Jones and what can I get for you today."

Fred turned away and dragging his feet along the ground, he went to talk to Chocolate Robin. "It's no good, Old Boy. I think we should pack up and go home. We're wasting our time and money."

Chocolate Robin brushed his scruffy mat of hair against Fred's legs and settled himself down under the table next to Fred's feet.

"Would you like to buy one of my sweets, Chocolate Robin?" asked Fred as he bent down again to talk to his friend. "I think you're the only one who's interested. I'll tell you what," he added as an afterthought, "why don't I give you one for free?"

"Good morning, Fred."

The sound of someone addressing him by his name startled him. It was Mrs. Jones, the lady the butcher had just been serving.

'Mr. Marlow tells me your sweets are very good and that I should taste one. It's really a bit early for me, and I have to confess, I'm not really a fan of chocolate. Perhaps you can advise me?"

"Do you like strawberries?" asked Fred, more out of good manners and politeness than from any hope of making a sale.

"I most certainly do," she replied and the smile that radiated across her face burst over Fred like the sun appearing from behind a storm cloud.

The joy in her voice lifted Fred's spirits. He picked up the plate of samples and presented it to her. He pointed to one of chocolates.

"This one's strawberry," he said, "but perhaps, you'd like to try something with a little more unusual taste; may I suggest…" He stopped himself short. He was about to go on when he realised he was gabbling nervously. He took a deep breath and tried to relax.

"I'll start with the strawberry, Fred, if you don't mind," and she picked up the small piece Fred indicated and popped it into her mouth.

"My word," she exclaimed, "Mr. Marlow was right. They are good."

Too nervous to watch Mrs. Jones's reaction, Fred concentrated his attention on Chocolate Robin. Apparently unconcerned with what was going on, he lay stretched out under the bench like a baby having its morning nap.

Mrs. Jones exclamation made Fred look up. His first thought was that she must not have liked it!

"Delicious!"

"Delicious? Did you say delicious?" asked Fred.

"I said delicious, and I meant just that."

It was all Fred could do not to run around to the other side of the bench to give her a hug.

"Thank you," he said. "Perhaps you'd like to try a different flavour. Let me surprise you. I won't tell you what it is, I'll let you guess."

He pointed to a Marmite flavoured one.

"Oh my," said Mrs. Jones as she tasted it. "This is unusual. It's like chocolate, and yet not chocolate." She gently moved the sweet inside her mouth, manipulating it with her tongue. "Whatever it is made of, it really is quite unusual as I said, but none the less delicious."

Fred explained that it was flavoured with Marmite, and he was about to go on to ask her if she would like to sample some of the other sweets he had, when she stopped him dead in his tracks.

"I'll buy a box of all six flavours," she said. "I'm sure my family will love them all."

Fred felt his eyes pop out of his head and land with a plop on the table in front of him. He gave himself a pinch to compose himself, picked up one of his variety boxes and handed it to her. "Thank you, Mrs. Jones. You are my first customer... after Mr. Marlow, that is."

He took the 50p she gave him and slipped it into his pocket. He tried not to smile but inside he was beaming.

It wasn't until after eight o'clock that trade picked up. From having been worried a couple of hours earlier that no one would buy his sweets, Fred ran into a much nicer problem; was he going to run out of sweets?

"Mr. Marlow," he said, taking an opportunity of a lull at both their stalls to go across and talk to him. "The sweets are selling so fast. Do you think I'm selling them too cheaply?"

"I was wondering that myself, Fred. There's only one way to find out; put up your prices and see!"

"But isn't that a bit like cheating?"

"There's no real answer to that. In business, it's never easy to know how much to charge. You want to get as much as possible, but at the same time, you don't want to upset your customers by charging too much. Why don't you finish early for lunch then come back this afternoon and try it out? You'll find the customers in the afternoon are different from the ones in the morning, and they won't know you've changed your prices, so hopefully, no one will get upset."

'Thanks, Mr. Marlow. I didn't have breakfast this morning and I could do with something to eat. I'll shut up shop now and go away and think about what you've said."

Fred and Chocolate Robin stopped at a small newsagent's, bought a sandwich and a drink, and strolled around the corner to the park where there was a drinking fountain especially for dogs.

"What do you think, Chocolate Robin? Am I being greedy if I put up my prices this afternoon? Would it be better to wait until next week?"

Fred felt his tummy rumble. He'd been too excited and too busy to have noticed how hungry he was.

"If I wait until next week, everyone will know I've put up my prices. If I do it this afternoon, it will only be the people who bought this morning who will know," he said talking out loud to himself.

Throughout the time it took him to eat his sandwich, Fred's mind turned over his dilemma time and time again.

"Oh, Chocolate Robin, making decisions can be so hard. I wish I knew what to do. It is obvious Uncle Victor and Aunty Nora haven't got enough money for themselves, never mind enough to look after me as well. If I can make a success of selling my sweets, I could help us out."

"Mr. Marlow," he said when he got back to the stall. "I'm going to be brave. I'm going to double my prices and see what happens."

"That sounds like a good idea, Fred. Good luck and keep smiling."

"I always try to do that, Mr. Marlow; it never feels nice when you're miserable."

Fred took several new pieces of card and some colourful crayons out of his bag and in his superist-bestest-most handwriting wrote:

Sweets 20p each,
Box of six £1.

"Here goes, Old Mate," he said to Chocolate Robin, "wish me luck."

He placed the cards prominently at the front of his stall and he waited to see what would happen.

Nothing happened…

Well nothing that hadn't happened that morning. He had as many customers in the afternoon as he'd had in the morning. In fact, if anything, he had more.

Mr. Marlow came across and whispered in Fred's ear, "Well done. How did you know that was the thing to do?"

"I didn't," replied Fred. "I asked Chocolate Robin."

"And I suppose he told you what to do?"

"Sort of," said Fred.

"And what type of 'sort of' was sort of?" replied Mr. Marlow recalling their first conversation together. And they both laughed.

Joe, the leader of the bullies, saw Fred selling his sweets and came over. He seemed genuinely pleased to see him.

"I was wondering if you'd be interested in asking my uncle to make you some fancy boxes to put the sweets into?" said Joe. "Your egg boxes are fun, but if you want to make a lot of money, it might be better to have posher looking ones."

Fred thought about it, but it was too far ahead for him to spend time on now and he was too busy at the moment. The only thoughts crowding his brain were things like, would anyone buy his sweets, and was he wasting his money. He thanked Joe for his suggestion and offered him a sweet.

"That's OK," said Joe. "I've just finished lunch. If there are any left-over, perhaps you could save me one for school tomorrow?"

Fred was surprised to hear Joe speaking like this. Gone was the bullying manner he carried around with him at school. In its place, he was as polite and normal as any other boy Fred had ever had as a friend.

"If you'd like," said Joe, "I can have a word with my uncle. He owns the factory that designs and makes the cardboard boxes. I'm sure he'll have lots of good ideas that might help you. It can't do any harm. The worst thing he can do is say no!"

Joe pulled a funny face as he pronounced the word 'no'. Fred guessed he was imitating the sound of Joe's uncle's voice, and they both laughed.

Joe said he'd hang around to help tidy up at the end of the day, but half an hour later, the last of the sweets were sold so there was nothing to be done.

"Well, I'll be off then," he said. "See you Monday."

Fred couldn't believe how magical his day had been. He'd forgotten all about how miserable he'd felt early in the day, and the rudeness of the young boy. And he'd forgotten about the anguish he'd gone through at lunch as he debated whether to put up his prices.

He sat down next to Chocolate Robin and wrapped his arms around him. "Thank you for your help and advice."

He stayed like this for a few moments, then got to his feet and strolled over to Mr. Marlow to ask if there was anything he could do to help him.

"No, Fred, there's not, but thank you for asking." Throughout the day, Mr. Marlow had kept an eye on what Fred had been doing. "I see you had a good day."

It was not a question he was asking, more of a comment, and yet somehow it was a question.

"I most certainly did," answered Fred. "And I want to thank you for your help."

"You did it all, Fred. There's no need to thank me." Something made the butcher turn to look at Chocolate Robin. "If you ask me," he continued, "it was Chocolate Robin who gave you advice. Could I borrow him sometimes to help me?"

Chocolate Robin, who'd been watching the two of them talk, turned his head in the other direction and went back to sleep.

Chapter 17
What to Do Next

So many exciting things had happened to him that day that Fred was still feeling elated when finally they reached home.

"Chocolate Robin, let me have your front paws. I'm so happy, I feel a Chocolate Robin song coming on."

Fred bent down, and with some difficulty, took hold of the sheep dog's front paws and lifted them up. With the dog standing upright onto its hind legs, and looking like a couple of fools, they danced around and around in circles whilst Fred sung out loud at the top of his voice.

"By golly, I needed that," he said when finally he deposited the dog back onto all fours. "It's lovely to sing Dad's song when you're feeling happy. Somehow it sounds different."

And with that, he grabbed hold of Chocolate Robin and they tumbled over and over on the ground as if rolling down a hill. They finally came to a halt when they collided with a bush.

Question after question crashed through Fred's mind like a river in flood.

"What shall I do now?" he asked. 'If I'm to be a success, I can't stop here. How many sweets should I make... and how many of each flavour?"

He looked up at the sky as he lay on his back and watched its blueness turn to bright red as evening set in. He couldn't remember feeling happier than this in all his life.

He thought about his arrival at his aunt and uncle's house, of his uncle's shouting, and his unfriendliness. True that hadn't changed but, feeling as he did now, none of that seemed to matter in the way that it had even a few hours earlier.

He looked at the house; his first description of it as looking like a 'shack' was quite a good one. And his room upstairs, even now that the rats had gone, was not something he wanted to think about, but his life was better than his Uncle Victor's. Because he was too big to get through the doorway, he was trapped inside the front room. The only chance he had of seeing the sun was if he poked his head out of the window.

I think I'd shout and scream a lot if I was in his position, he thought, *added to that they seem to have very little money to live on, almost no furniture, and certainly no bath.* Perhaps his uncle's complaining was in some strange way his way of cheering himself up?

"Chocolate Robin, you haven't fallen asleep again, have you?" he asked when he heard his friend snore. "I forgot to ask Mr. Marlow for some more egg boxes. I won't be able to make more sweets tonight if I've nothing to put them in."

Fred's mind started racing again. Like a tide ebbing and flowing, ideas bounced backwards and forwards from one side of his head to the other.

Chocolate Robin was lying on his side with his tongue hanging out. He was blissfully asleep.

Fred gave him a push.

"Hoy," he said. "Wake up! I need your advice."

The dog yawned, let out a sigh and turned as if to face Fred.

"I've been thinking. Do you remember Joe's idea about getting his uncle to design and make us some fancy boxes to put the sweets in? What do you think? I'm worried they'll be too expensive. Do you think it's too early for us to spend money on that? Imagine how much we'd waste if no one is interested?"

It began to rain.

"I'm going in now," said Fred. "I'll see you tomorrow and we'll go over everything again. Oh, by the way," he added as he rolled over off his back and stood up, "Mr. Marlow gave me a piece of beef to cook tonight. I don't know if you're interested but he threw in a couple of Tyrannosaurus Rex bones for you."

At the sound of the word 'bones', Chocolate Robin jumped up onto his feet and barked twice in quick succession.

"A double woof is not good enough to get Tyrannosaurus Rex bones," said Fred. "I expect at least a triple woof!"

The dog did not oblige but simply stood there with his tail wagging and his mouth open. As he looked up at Fred, blobs of saliva ran down his tongue and dripped onto the grass like a leaky tap.

"Can you do me a favour?" said Fred as he fished the bones out of the bag and gave them to the dog. "Try and think up a few more flavours for the sweets. If we're to be a success, we need something extra special. Something that makes our sweets different from any others anywhere in the world."

And with that, he climbed up the ladder and into the house.

"I'll take ideas from you too, Owlie," he said as the barn owl, perched on the roof top, caught his eye.

On his way down the ladder to the kitchen to put the beef into the fridge, Fred nearly collided with Aunty Nora as she came out of the front room.

"Did you have a nice day, Fred?"

"Yes, I did, thank you, Aunt. But I've run out of egg boxes. You don't happen to have any I can put my sweets into if I make some tonight?"

From the expression on Aunty Nora's face, he could see the answer was no. But then if he'd stopped to think first, he'd have known that without asking the question. Why did he keep opening his big trap? If his legs had have been long enough, Fred would have kicked himself for having asked. He wanted to crawl away and disappear back up to his room.

To change the subject he said, "What were you thinking of eating tonight?" and then wished he hadn't said that either.

"I haven't had a chance to get to the shops today," she replied. "Would you like some of those eggs you bought? We could scramble them on toast. I think we've got enough bread."

He was about to say he had some beef he could roast tonight, but cut himself off when he realised it would have been rude, now that his aunt had come up with a suggestion.

"I got some roast beef off Mr. Marlow, the butcher," he said as casually as he could.

He chose his words carefully. He knew what he'd said wasn't strictly true, but it wasn't a lie either. Phrasing it the way he had, he hoped his aunt would think he'd bought it. He knew she'd be upset if she thought the butcher was giving them meat as charity.

"Perhaps we could have the roast beef tomorrow with Yorkshire pudding and some vegetables?"

"Roast beef!" she replied. "We haven't had roast beef for ages. That would be lovely." *And so would scrambled eggs*, thought Fred, *for that would free up an egg box for me to put my sweets in. I can use a baking tray to stack some others on.*

He made a note to get up early the next day and go to the supermarket. Perhaps, he'd come up with some ideas there.

Fred wanted to know how much money he'd made that day but was too nervous and excited to check; nervous in case he hadn't made as much as he hoped, excited in case he'd made more. He promised himself he'd count it after he'd gone up to bed.

Chapter 18
Sunday Is a Day of Rest (Part 1)

Fred was tired after the excitement of his day and promised himself a Sunday morning lie in.

Owlie had other ideas. The moment the sun rose above the horizon, the owl landed with a bump on the frame of the attic window.

Hearing the sudden noise, and fearing the rats had returned to attack him *en masse*, Fred woke up with a start. Eyes darting in all directions, he scoured his floor for any signs of them. Relieved he could see nothing untoward, he chanced to look up and saw Owlie draping strings of what looked like pieces of weed or fungus over the top of the frame of the window. Too tired to take much notice, Fred turned over to go back to sleep.

A few minutes later, with a flutter and a bump, the owl returned, carrying more strings of what looked like the same stuff. Carefully placing them one at a time next to the ones it had brought earlier, it flew off again.

Every ten minutes or so, it returned with more and more of the weed-like substance until, by the time Fred could get up enough energy to drag himself out of bed and go to have a look, the whole of the left hand side of the window was covered in a curtain of green.

He strolled over to the window to have a closer look at what was going on.

The weed looked like some form of fungus or algae, but not really knowing what weed, fungus, and algae were—they might have been all the same for all he knew—he could safely say he'd never seen anything like it before.

Soft and a bit wet and spongy to the touch, like seaweed, the only remarkable thing about it was that it didn't appear to have a smell.

Fred was busily poking and feeling it when the owl returned with another beak-full. Expecting the owl to land on the roof nearby and wait for him to move away from the window, he was surprised when it continued its flight and landed right next to him.

"Good morning, Owlie?" he said in as quiet a voice he could muster, so as not to startle it. "And what do you think you're doing? Are you making me some curtains?"

The owl, much as Chocolate Robin did, ignored him. It got on with its job of laying the fungus on top of the others and then flew off towards a part of the wood further down the lane.

Fred caught sight of Chocolate Robin sitting in the garden. He was looking up and appeared to be watching what was going on.

"Stay there," shouted Fred. "I'm coming. I'll grab some cornflakes and bring them down. Perhaps you can tell me what Owlie's up to?"

In too much of a hurry to put his blankets on top of the inflatable bed, Fred rushed down to the kitchen to get his cornflakes. Balancing the bowl in one hand and using his other to hold onto the ladder, he climbed back up into the attic.

He was crossing his room towards the window when he remembered he ought to tell his aunt he was going to have his breakfast in the garden and wouldn't be eating with them that morning.

In a great hurry at his sudden excitement for the day ahead, he put the bowl down on the floor, spun around, put one foot on each side of the ladder, and slid down the ladder like a fireman sliding down a pole.

His descent was much quicker than he'd thought. He lost control and landed with an almighty thump. His legs gave way beneath him and tumbling over, he crashed into the living room door, smashing it open.

When he thought about it afterwards, Fred felt he'd been a bit unlucky. For one thing, what were the chances of Uncle Victor being up and on his feet? For the second, what were the chances that at that very moment, his uncle would be standing just behind the door?

All the time and effort Fred had put into trying to win over his uncle in the hope he'd get him to like him just a little bit in return, disappeared like a puff of smoke in a gale. The full force of the door smacked into Uncle Victor, knocking him backwards.

Sprawled on his back, Fred looked up. He couldn't believe his eyes. The force of the door smashing into his uncle's body had set it wobbling like an enormous jelly on a plate. Tidal waves of fat were racing across him in all directions like tsunamis hurtling across vast oceans. Huge waves of skin, rising and falling like seagulls battered in a storm, cascaded over his chest and down his arms with ever increasing fury. Waves of fat on their way up met others on their way down. Undulations flowing round his belly in one direction crashed into others on their way back. Wherever they collided there were kafuffles. Like great armies locked in combat, they bumped and bustled, wiggled and wobbled, jiggled and joggled, as they strived for victory on the field of battle.

Uncle Victor was stuck in the middle. Hapless, he had no control over what was happening. Looking like a huge blob quivering with delight, his body shook in time to their motion.

Fred watched as a small part of a wave broke off and went on an adventure of its own. Jiggling its way up his neck, it rippled across his cheek, forcing his left eyelid to shut as it passed. By the time it reached his uncle's other eye, its momentum was slowing. Not having enough energy to close the second eyelid, it crashed into the eyeball, sending it rocking backwards and forwards like the pendulum in a grandfather clock.

A dazed Uncle Victor opened his closed eye. Peering out in the direction of his nephew sprawled on the ground, it failed to see him. All it could see was the forest of hair sprouting from the end of his own nose. The force of impact made by the door had knocked the eyeball so far into the corner of its socket that it had taken up home and was nesting there. His other eye, the one that had been bouncing from side to side, decided to change its motion and was now whizzing around and around in circles, emitting rainbows of light as it did so.

Fred stared up at his uncle in a mixture of shock, awe, and amazement. Not knowing which eye to focus on, he concentrated first on the left, then on the right, and then back again, until he became dizzy trying to keep up.

"Sorry, Uncle Victor," he blurted as his innate animal instinct took over, and not waiting for an answer, he picked himself up and made a mad dash for the ladder and the safety of the attic.

Calming himself as best he could, he grabbed his bowl of cornflakes and set off across the attic to join Chocolate Robin in the garden.

It was only when he reached the window that he realised he had another problem. Not a great one it should be said, and certainly nothing to compare with what he'd created with his uncle, but a problem all the same. How was he to climb out of the attic window and down the ladder carrying his bowl of cornflakes without spilling the milk?

"Easy peazy, Chocolate Robin. Watch this!"

Fred put the bowl of cereal on the ledge of the window and squeezed out past it. He settled his feet on a rung of the ladder, reached back to pick up the bowl, and stopped to think.

Perhaps it would be best to balance the bowl on his head like he'd seen ladies sometimes do when carrying baskets in films?

Or perhaps he could try tucking it under his arm?

Or perhaps he should forget about it and leave it on the window ledge. He could always have breakfast in town.

In the end, he decided to carry it in one hand and hope for the best.

As luck would have it, the best happened and he made it down into the garden without spilling a drop.

"As I said, Chocolate Robin, easy peazy. And I thought you said it was impossible! Look at that, not a drop spilt."

The dog wasn't bothered whether it was impossible or not.

Outside in the fresh air, all thoughts about Uncle Victor and what might happen when he had to turn up for breakfast the following day disappeared from Fred's mind. Tomorrow was another day. He had a lot to do before then.

"Look, Chocolate Robin there's Owlie, coming back with another beak full of fungus. What's he up to?"

Fred paused as he ate his cornflakes and, forgetting his mouth was still full, continued speaking.

"I must…"

He had to stop in mid-sentence to swallow the mush that filled his mouth. "I must get some egg boxes from somewhere this morning. If I don't, I won't have anywhere to put the sweets I want to make today. The thing is…"

He stuffed another spoonful of flakes into his mouth, chewed them a couple of time, and swallowed them.

"As I said yesterday, I've no idea where I can get any. It's Sunday today so Mr. Marlow's shop will be closed and, as I haven't the foggiest clue where he lives, I can't go round to his house to ask him for some.

"I could try the supermarket I suppose. Do you think they'd let me empty the eggs out of their eggs boxes? I could arrange them neatly on the shelves so people reach them easily. That way they could pick however many they wanted. They might like that! I mean, why do we have to buy eggs in sixes, it doesn't make sense to me?"

Chocolate Robin, who'd been sitting on his hind legs minding his own business, got up onto his feet and set off towards the garden gate as if he was going somewhere.

"I'll take that as a no," shouted Fred when he saw his friend wander off. "What's up? Have you got ants in your pants?"

Realising he was not being followed, the dog stopped, turned around, and gave a bark. He waited until he had Fred's attention, then hopped over what used to be the gate and set off down the lane. He headed in the direction of the woods from where Owlie appeared to be collecting his weed.

"Hold on. I'm coming," shouted Fred. "Let me have a few more mouthfuls of cornflakes. I'm starving." And with that, he stuffed three large spoonfuls of flakes into his mouth and, using the back of his hand as a cloth, wiped away the milk dribbling from his mouth.

Now that Fred was following him, Chocolate Robin set off down the lane at a brisk pace just as Owlie was returning with another string of fungus.

"Here I am, getting the sheep to tidy up the front garden," chuntered Fred as he trundled down the lane after

119

his four legged friend, "and there's Owlie, bringing in fungus by the beakful, messing things up again!"

Chapter 19
Sunday Is a Day of Rest (Part 2)

About a mile or so down the lane from the cottage, was a clearing in the wood. A long driveway wound its way towards a house that was set well back from the road. Like large flecks of dandruff blowing around the house, hundreds of chickens were pecking the ground in search of food and enjoying the sunshine.

Chocolate Robin hopped over the entrance gate to the house as if he owned the place. Hesitant and surprised, and not knowing what else to do, Fred copied him.

An elderly lady, wearing a pinafore, saw them approach and came out of the house. It looked as if she'd been cooking, for she was brushing the flour off her hands as she came towards them.

"I know who you are," she said, looking at Fred. "You were the boy at the market yesterday, selling those sweets. What can I do for you?"

Fred had no idea what she could do for him, for he didn't know why they were there. All he was doing was following Chocolate Robin. He thought the dog must have lived here, but he could see by the reaction of the woman that this was not the case.

After rather a long pause whilst he thought of what he could say without making too much of a fool of himself, he answered, "I'm not sure why I'm here," making a fool of himself.

"I was just following my dog," he continued. "He seemed to know where he was going, but I can see now that he didn't."

Chocolate Robin turned his head and looked up at Fred as if in disbelief.

Suddenly an idea came into Fred's head and without thinking he blurted out, "Have you got any egg boxes I can buy off you?"

"Well, that's an unusual request I have to say," answered the lady and gave a big smile. "I've never had anyone come here to buy egg boxes. There's a first time for everything as my mother used to say."

Fred thought he should explain his apparent rudeness, but as usual, he got tongue tied and started to ramble on. Not sure he would ever finish telling her why he was there, the woman cut him off to save him further embarrassment.

"Of course, you can buy some egg boxes," she said. "Your luck is in. I use hundreds of them each day and only yesterday, I took delivery of a new lot. How many would you like?"

"How many can I have?" said Fred a bit sheepishly, for he had no idea how many to ask for.

"Ten? Twenty?" she replied. "Fifty?"

"Oh yes, fifty! Fifty will keep me going until Monday."

"In that case, you'd better take a hundred, and you can keep going until Tuesday," she said and flashed him another smile.

"Thanks, a hundred," said Fred and they both laughed at his nonsense.

The old lady wouldn't let Fred give her any money.

"I buy so many boxes I get a good price. A hundred boxes cost me very little; it wouldn't be worth my while to take the money off you. I'll tell you what, next time I see you at the market, you can give me a sweet for free, how about that?"

"It's a deal," replied Fred.

The old lady came back with a couple of big carrier bags overflowing with egg boxes. She gave them to Fred and she waved to them as they set off back out on the lane.

"Now where was it you were taking me before we wound up in the old lady's garden?"

But Chocolate Robin seemed to have lost interest and turned back up the lane towards Appletree Cottage. Fred guessed the dog must be getting old and had forgotten why they'd come here.

On the way home, they spotted Owlie high up in a tree, tugging on a tangle of fungus hanging next to a large clump of mistletoe. It took him a while to unravel it and pull it free. He was so busy with what he was doing he didn't seem to have noticed them.

"Chocolate Robin, I'm sure Owlie's up to something."

On their way back, one of the carrier bags burst so Fred had to try to carry half of the egg boxes in his arms. A few fell onto the road. As his way of helping Chocolate Robin, picked them up in his mouth.

Fred, who didn't want to tell the dog about hygiene and explain that he wouldn't be able to use those two boxes, had a great idea.

I know how I can use those boxes, he thought, *I'll put Uncle Victor's sweets in them!*

He didn't really mean it…

Or did he? He wasn't sure.

The barn owl had taken up residence on the frame of the attic window as if it was its home. It seemed to wait until Fred had put the egg boxes down and then flew down and landed on the grass next to him. In its beak, it was carrying a long string of fungus. The owl carefully placed the fungus on the ground in front of Fred and then flew back up to his new-found perch on top of the window.

"What's Owlie up to?" asked Fred who, now that the owl had flown away, felt he could move again.

"Why's he done that?"

As Fred often did, he asked the second question without waiting for an answer to the first.

"I'm not going to pick it up for him if that's what he wants. And if he thinks I'm going to throw him the fungus so he can chase after it and bring it back, he's got another thing coming. He's not a dog."

Chocolate Robin went up to the fungus and pushing it with his front paw, moved it closer to Fred.

"Don't you start, I'm not going to throw it for you either; I've got cooking to do!"

Chocolate Robin gave a bark, picked up the fungus in his mouth and placed it on top of Fred's foot.

"I'm not playing football either. I haven't time for games now!"

Fred flicked his foot up into the air and watched the fungus pirouette and float down back onto the grass. He bent down, picked up an armful of boxes, and set off to climb up the ladder. But that was as far as he got, for Chocolate Robin was blocking his path.

"Get out of my way, Old Mate!" said Fred, trying to control his patience.

Chocolate Robin stood his ground.

"I've told you, I'm not in the mood for playing games. If I'm to make a success of making sweets, I have to do just that… make sweets. Now let me pass."

As Fred finished speaking, the owl launched itself off the roof, brushing Fred's hair with its wing tips as it passed. Without landing on the grass, it scooped up the piece of fungus from off the ground and dropped it on top of the egg boxes Fred was carrying.

"What do you think you're doing?" cried Fred, startled both by the sudden appearance of the owl and being bombed.

"Whatever silly game you two are playing with your slimy piece of fungus, will you please stop it? I'm not going to throw it to you. And if you think I'm going to put it into my mouth, like you do, then think again. I'm not French you know."

As he said these words, Fred stopped. He looked at Chocolate Robin and then up at Owlie circling above.

"No," he said. "No, no, no!"

The owl swooped around and plucked the fungus back off the top of the boxes. He carried it up to the attic window and draped it over the others.

"You're not trying to tell me I should eat it. Are you?"

There was a long moment of silence whilst the three of them looked at each other.

"Ok, ok! But no disrespect, fellas. I'm not going to eat it… but I know someone who will."

A huge grin spread across Fred's face.

"Uncle Victor!"

Fred knew he shouldn't think things like that, not even in fun, but he couldn't help himself.

"He'll eat it! He'll eat anything. I'll let him be the guinea pig. I'll put some on his dinner plate tonight and pretend it's a new sort of cabbage. He gulps everything down so quickly, he won't even notice he's eaten it. Who knows," he added, "I might even give it to him raw!"

Fred was so busy 'cooking up' his plan he hadn't noticed that Chocolate Robin had moved out of his way and was now lying on the grass.

"I'll see you guys in the morning," he shouted and began the first of several journeys carrying the egg boxes up to his room.

Chapter 20
The Fungus

It was as if Fred's aunt had been waiting for his return, for no sooner had he descended the ladder from the attic and entered the kitchen than she appeared out of the gloom behind him.

"I've never seen your uncle so angry. He wants to see you as soon as you come in."

"I had a feeling he might," replied Fred. "Is he hurt?"

As the words slipped out of his mouth, he realised it was another silly thing to have said. He was getting tired of keep telling himself to think before speaking. Of course his uncle was hurt, he'd just been whacked by a door, hadn't he? His eyes were probably still looping the loop and flashing all the colours of the rainbow.

"He says he is, but I'm not quite sure," she replied a little doubtfully. "But whether he is or is not, I don't think it's a good idea for you to see him right now. It's best you stay out of the way. Try not to make any noise. There could be trouble if he hears you're back. Let's hope he calms down a bit by the morning."

"Thanks, Aunty. I'll be as quiet as I can."

Since leaving the house that morning, Fred had forgotten all about the accident he'd had with Uncle Victor.

"Tell you what, why don't I cook us a special meal for tonight? Along with the lovely piece of beef to roast, I've got a special vegetable I'm sure Uncle Victor would enjoy."

As he spoke, it was all Fred could do to keep a straight face.

"That sounds wonderful, Fred. But there's a problem. If you cook it, he'll know you're back. I'll tell you what, you cook it but I'll come out from time to time to pretend I'm doing it."

"Good idea, aunty. That delicious vegetable I was telling you about, I'm afraid I've only got enough for Uncle Victor. It's a shame but you and I will have to go without. Please don't tell him about it. I want it to be his surprise. You don't mind, do you?"

"Oh, you are a thoughtful boy. I'm sure it will cheer your uncle up."

"It's a shame he won't let me eat dinner with you. I'd love to see the pleasure on his face when he tastes it. I'm sure he'll be bowled over."

The rest of the day was all work. Fred's priority was to make his sweets and he was pleased with how many he'd packed into the egg boxes, by the time it was time to make the supper.

In her attempt to convince Uncle Victor she was preparing the meal, Aunty Nora made regular visits to the kitchen. She was amazed how much at ease Fred was, doing the cooking. She had difficulty boiling an egg without it ending up too runny or too hard.

"And now for the magic ingredient," said Fred to himself when she left to set the table. "To make sure he doesn't notice it and refuses to try it, I'll mix it in amongst his other vegetables. I think I'll dry a small bit of the weed in the oven, then crush it up into a dust and sprinkle it over his meat; if he does see it he'll think it's just pepper."

The next time his aunt returned to the kitchen, everything was ready and on the plates.

"This one is for Uncle Victor," said Fred.

"And this must be the vegetable you were talking about. It looks a little like spinach, doesn't it? I don't think I've ever seen it before. What's it called?"

"I'm not sure what its name is," replied Fred. "I suppose it must have one."

"What shall I tell Uncle Victor if he asks?"

"He may not notice it, but if he does, tell him it's a form of cabbage?"

"That's a good idea. He likes cabbage."

"Then I'm sure he'll like this."

Fred turned his head away to hide his smile and waited until his aunt had taken their meals and closed the living room door. He tiptoed over to listen to his uncle's reaction.

"WHERE IS HE?" roared his uncle.

"What do you mean, Victor, where is he?"

"THE BOY! THE IDIOT! THE GOOD-FOR-NOTHING!"

"Try not to get upset again, Victor. Eat your dinner whilst it's still hot. I've gone to a lot of trouble making it for you."

"Don't try and tell me you cooked this, Nora," he said. "I may look a fool, but I'm not."

Fred would have loved to have answered, twisted his uncle's words just a little, but he held his breath and kept listening.

"Eat up, Victor. I don't know about you but I'm hungry."

From the sounds of chomping, Fred could tell his uncle didn't wait to be asked a second time.

"Is that pepper you've put on the meat, Vera?"

"I'm not sure dear. Perhaps I did. I know you like a little pepper on your meat."

"But that's the point, it's not a little. It looks like you spilt it."

"Oh dear, did I? Perhaps you'd like to swop plates with me?"

Fred could feel himself wanting to shout out 'no!' and try to stop her. His master plan was in danger of going terribly wrong and he was helpless to do anything about it; to go in now risked ruining everything.

"Why don't you taste it, dear? I'm sure you'll like it."

There was a brief moment of silence.

"It doesn't smell like pepper."

"I'm not sure pepper has much of a smell," replied his wife.

"And it doesn't taste like pepper."

"If you don't like it, dear, as I said, we can swop plates."

"I'm not swopping plates. Whatever it is, it's delicious. Get me some more!"

Fred stood back from the door and rushed into the kitchen to await the arrival of his aunt.

"I'm sorry," said Fred in answer to her question, "but I don't have any more. Why not tell him you knocked the rest over and it fell in the sink? I'll make sure I get some more for him tomorrow."

Her return to the front room was greeted by howls of shouting from his uncle. "Then make sure I have some more tomorrow."

"And what's this green mush?" he asked, pointing at the cooked fungus.

"It's a new form of cabbage."

"Well, it doesn't look like it. And where's yours? How come you don't have any? Are you trying to poison me?"

"The cabbage was expensive, Victor. I wanted it to be a treat for you. There was only enough money to buy a small amount. I know how much you like cabbage."

Good old Aunty, thought Fred. *You'd make a super saleswoman, couldn't have done better myself.*

The suspense of not being able to see what was going on was nearly killing him. His aunt had done a terrific selling job but would his uncle take the bait and eat it. He wished the door had been made of one way glass so that he could have watched. All he could do was imagine.

Will he?
Won't he?
Will he?
Won't he?

"Vera!" screamed his uncle in a voice that Fred had never heard before. "My goodness, Vera. What was that I just ate?"

He's dying, thought Fred. *I've killed him.*

He grabbed hold of the door handle to rush in and stopped himself. *Think before speaking, think before acting,* he was beginning to learn.

And what would he say if he went in? 'Sorry Uncle, I didn't mean to kill you this time either, it was just a joke'.

"MORE! I WANT SOME MORE!"

He was still alive. The great bull elephant was back and bellowing for more. He loved it. OLIVER TWIST LOVED IT!

"But there is no more, Victor. I told you I only had enough money to buy a little and I gave it all to you."

"Vera," he replied, in yet another strange voice that Fred had never heard before. "You're wonderful. Now I know why I married you."

"Thank you, Victor. But perhaps you should really be thanking Fred. It was his idea."

"FRED? FRED? DON'T TELL ME THAT BOY HAD SOMETHING TO DO WITH THIS! You wait till I get my hands on him."

"But Victor…"

Chapter 21
Things Start to Move

Hearing his uncle's reaction to eating the fungus and how delicious he thought it was, Fred was tempted to try some for himself, but remembering how horrible it looked he had no trouble persuading himself not to.

The following morning, he rose early and using the excuse that he had a lot to do, he tapped on his aunt's bedroom door and explained that he was going to school early and would not have time to eat breakfast with them.

What Fred had said was true but, after yesterday's unfortunate incident with the living room door, what was also true was that he was in no rush to see his uncle.

With as many egg boxes of sweets as he could pack into his rucksack, he set off to see Mr. Marlow to talk business. Chocolate Robin must have known Fred was going to set off early, for he was sitting in the garden waiting for him.

Mr. Marlow was delighted to see them both and even more so when he saw how many boxes of sweets Fred had brought for him to sell.

"It's early days, Fred," he said, "but even my son is convinced that having your sweets on sale has brought us more customers."

"That's nice to hear, Mr. Marlow. Have you got a few minutes so we can talk about what I should do next. You see, I think I need a bank account and I don't know how to set one up. Perhaps I'm too young to have one?"

"I don't think you can be too young," replied Mr. Marlow, "but it might be a good idea to get your mam or dad to open one with you."

Fred felt he had to explain to the butcher that he didn't have any parents. He felt embarrassed telling him that he was living with his aunt and uncle but was pleased that Mr. Marlow didn't seem bothered. He even thought of joking that his uncle could go with him—but that it might be difficult for he would have to carry the house with him!

"I'm sure Aunty Nora will come with me."

They agreed a price for the next lot of sweets and calculated how much the total came to. It seemed like a lot of money. Mr. Marlow went behind the counter to get it from the till when Chocolate Robin suddenly appeared in the doorway.

"Outside, Boy!" commanded Fred. "You know you're not allowed in here."

Fred took the money from Mr. Marlow's outstretched hand and thrust it into his pocket, but as he did so, he was surprised to hear Chocolate Robin let out a low growl.

"Thanks, Mr. Marlow. I'll call in tonight on my way back from school and see how the sale of the sweets went." He turned to leave.

"Chocolate Robin," said Fred, "you're blocking the way."

Chocolate Robin refused to budge.

"Move over, I said. You're being awkward again."

Fred tried to push his way past the dog but he wasn't strong enough to move him.

"If it's bones you're after, it's too early. We'll get some for you when we come back in the evening."

Chocolate Robin was having nothing of it and continued to block the doorway.

"What's up with you? You did the same thing in the garden yesterday. Move over. There's a good dog, you're in the way."

Chocolate Robin let out another low growl.

Like in the garden the day before, Fred began to get impatient. He had no idea what to do. He felt embarrassed in front of the butcher. With Chocolate Robin blocking the doorway, not only could Fred not get out but customers could not get in. Luckily, it was still early in the morning and no one was around.

"I don't know what the matter is, Mr. Marlow. I've never seen him behave like this," he said, not wishing to waste time explaining that the dog, and the owl (when he came to think about it), had done the same sort of thing the day before.

"He's unhappy about something, Fred. Something's bothering him."

Mr. Marlow made his way around from behind the counter.

"Let me have a chat with him."

Fred stepped back to let Mr. Marlow pass.

"What is it, old boy? What's troubling you?"

He bent down, reached out his hand and patted Chocolate Robin. The dog seemed happy to be stroked and looked at the butcher.

"What are you trying to tell us? Are you unhappy with Fred carrying all that money to school? Is that the problem? Let's see if that's what it is."

The butcher stood up.

"Fred," he said, "give me the money back for a moment and we'll see what the dog does."

It seemed like a daft idea but Fred thought it could do no harm. He handed the money back to Mr. Marlow and as he did so, Chocolate Robin turned around and went outside to wait.

"That's amazing," said the butcher. "Your dog's right, you know. We should have thought of that. It's not a good idea for you go to school carrying lots of money. Who knows what might happen if people find out. I'll give it to you when you come back after school and you can take it straight home.

"Oh, and you're right about the bank account," he added as Fred was about to leave the shop. "The sooner you set one up, the better. When you've got an account, I can transfer your money straight into it. You won't need to carry it."

On their way to school, Fred thought about how strange Chocolate Robin was for a dog. It was as if he knew what was best for Fred. Sometimes he even felt the dog knew what Fred was thinking.

A few hundred yards from the entrance to the playground, Chocolate Robin stopped and with a goodbye bark, turned off into a nearby field. Fred had no idea what the dog did whilst he went to school, but he knew that somehow he would not be far away when he was needed.

Joe was leaning against the school gate as Fred arrived. He too must have got up early and was bubbling with ideas.

He fished into the bag he was carrying and pulled out some attractively coloured pieces of cardboard.

"These fold into boxes," he said. "I told my uncle about your sweets, and how you were using egg boxes to keep them in, and he came up with these as an idea."

Rather than look at them in full view of everyone coming to school, they went off to the back of the bicycle sheds.

The cardboard was of very good quality, smooth to touch, and although quite thin, it was strong. Mainly light blue in colour, the boxes had occasional red swirls of different thicknesses that caught the eye and made you look at them.

"He's made three different sorts," said Joe. "He liked your idea of putting them in egg boxes, but he felt that if your sweets were as expensive tasting as I told him they were, they should be sold in boxes that look expensive. He says packaging is everything in business... but then he would, wouldn't he? ... that's how he makes his money."

Fred smiled. He took the pieces of card Joe handed to him and folded them to make boxes. It was love at first sight. He couldn't believe that one day, he might be selling his sweets in them. He took some of his sweets out of the egg boxes and placed them delicately inside the new packages. They fitted perfectly. Joe's uncle knew what he was doing.

"I love them," said Fred. "Can I take them home with me? I need time to think over how I would like them decorated. I would like to have a catchy logo… one that will tell people at a glance where they come from. Oh, and I'll have to find a special name for them," he added as an afterthought.

Chapter 22
A Turn for the Worse

"Why don't we sell a few of your sweets at break time?" said Joe. "We'll test the market. We won't be able to charge the same prices you can get from grown-ups, but it will let you experiment with new flavours and ideas."

"I'm not sure I want to do that," replied Fred. "I think we'd better ask if that's allowed. I wouldn't want to get into trouble, especially as I've only just arrived."

"Perhaps it's allowed and perhaps it isn't," said Joe with a smile, "but you know what they say. 'What the eye doesn't see' and all that. Trust me, Fred, no one will see us, and if they do," he added, "what harm can we be doing? We're just selling a few sweets. We'll say we didn't know and apologise and that will be the end of it."

"I'm not sure," said Fred. "If I'm going to sell them at school, I'd rather wait until after school's finished."

"Trust me, Fred. I've done this sort of thing before. If we go and sell them behind the bicycle sheds, no one will see us. We're well hidden there."

Fred wasn't convinced but because Joe was so enthusiastic and, for the sake of the bullying, he agreed; and after all, he needed Joe if he was going to get his uncle to make the new boxes. He didn't feel he could say 'no'. What harm could there be?

Fred had so many things on his mind, he didn't pay much attention to the lessons before break. As soon as the bell sounded, Joe came across to talk to him.

"What price were you thinking of selling them for?" he asked.

"Forty pence each, sixty pence for two," replied Fred.

"That's far too much," said Joe. "It's twice the price you were selling them for in the market. You're selling to kids at school, you know. Twenty pence each would be the topside."

"I've thought about it," said Fred sticking to his guns. "That's my price. I'm not selling them for less."

Joe was about to argue but could see from the way Fred had spoken that he wasn't going to change his mind. What Joe didn't understand was the true reason why Fred had set the price so high; something deep inside told him that what they were going to do was not a good idea.

"You sell them," said Fred, "I'll stand at the back and watch. That way, I can study the reaction of the buyers. It'll give me a good idea of what they like best and how much they're willing to pay."

Word quickly got around that Fred's sweets were up for sale and a stampede started. Kids swarmed around the area of the bike sheds, some to buy and others just to see what was happening.

A secondary market set up. Enterprising kids were buying two sweets for sixty pence and undercutting the market by selling them on at thirty five pence each; making ten pence profit every time they did it. There was nothing Fred could do to stop it. It was like having lit the blue touch paper on a firework and not being able step backwards to avoid the blast.

Within minutes, there were so many kids hanging around the bicycle sheds that the teachers on duty couldn't ignore it and came across to see what was happening. Sensing trouble, Joe's gang tried to warn them but Joe, trapped inside the crowd, couldn't escape. The teachers took hold of him and marched him off into the school. The few boxes he hadn't yet sold were confiscated.

Fred was in a quandary. Not knowing what to do, he milled around the school yard like a dog that had lost its bone. "What had happened had happened," he told himself, and for the moment, there was nothing he could do.

When the bell sounded for the end of break, he made his way back to the classroom. Joe's desk was empty.

"Fred Smith?" called the teacher. "I've just asked you a question. What's the answer?"

"Forty two," said Fred without thinking.

"Forty two! Forty two! Since when has forty two been the name of the largest country in the world? You're in a geography lesson boy, not maths!"

Fred could see the teacher was not amused.

"How about you do a little extra work after school? Stay behind for half an hour. I will not put up with such behaviour. Why don't we…"

But before the teacher could say any more, the classroom door opened and Mr. Jones, the headmaster, walked in. A giant of a man; his shadow and silence fell across the class.

"I'm sorry to interrupt your lesson, Mr. Brown," he said, "but I wonder if you'd mind if I took Fred Smith out of your class; I would like to have a discussion with him."

"Certainly, Headmaster, be my guest. I fear young Smith may be what one calls a bit of a nuisance. Today was our first lesson and I've already felt it necessary to give him a detention for his poor behaviour."

"Thank you, Mr. Brown. I'll bear that in mind when Smith and I have our chat." The headmaster turned towards Fred. "Follow me boy."

When they arrived at the Headmaster's study, Joe was standing outside, his head bent forward as if examining his shoes to see how dirty they were. There was no smile on his face. He deliberately avoided looking at Fred

"Come in, both of you," said the headmaster.

He showed them to the front of his desk, walked around to the other side, and sat himself down. He paused for a moment as if contemplating then looked up.

"Now, Fred," he said looking him straight in the face, "I've been having a little chat with Joe here about selling sweets on the school premises. You do know that it's not allowed don't you?"

From the way the headmaster had phrased the question, Fred knew he was supposed to answer yes.

"No, I didn't know that, Headmaster."

He said it respectfully and tried to keep his voice calm. He spoke in a neutral way so as not to annoy the head; he didn't want to make matters worse.

"Well, let me tell you that it is… and that we deal with such breaches of the school rules very seriously, very seriously indeed."

He paused but never once took his eyes off Fred.

"Now, I know that you are new here, Fred, and I was prepared to give you the benefit of the doubt…"

What doubt? thought Fred. *How was I to know it was against the school rules?*

"I've already had a chat with Joe here and, knowing Joe as I do, I have no reason to doubt what he has told me."

Fred was relieved to hear these words. He knew Joe would have stuck up for him and have explained what happened. It had been—he searched for a word—unfortunate, yes unfortunate, that sounded like a good word to use if he was asked.

"There's only one way I can see what you've been doing, Fred," continued the head standing up and towering above him. He slid his glasses down to the end of his nose and peered down at Fred over the top of them.

"Let me get straight to the point. You bullied Joe here into doing your selling for you. Whilst he was made to look like the front man, you hung around out of sight at the back. It is quite obvious to me…" He turned and looked towards Joe, "knowing Joe as I do…"

The headmaster turned back to look at Fred.

"As I was saying," he continued, "it is obvious to me that you, and you alone, are the guilty party. I don't know what hold you have over Joe that made him do it against his will but in my books, getting someone else to do your dirty

140

work is bullying. Bullying is something we take very seriously and cannot ignore!"

Each word the headmaster said sounded louder in Fred's head than the last. They became so loud he wanted to put his hands over his ears to drown out the noise. He could feel Joe squirming nervously beside him. He wanted to tell him exactly what he thought; that he'd been sold down the river; that Joe was a bully, and like all bullies, he was soft and when threatened saved his own skin first; that if anyone stood up to him with equal force he'd run away.

"Have you anything to say in your defence?" continued the headmaster in a slightly quieter voice.

What could Fred say? It was obvious the headmaster had already made up his mind. It was Fred's word against Joe's. Even if he tried to argue about who said what, and when, and to whom, he couldn't get around the fact that the sweets were his. Everyone knew that. That, at least, was a fact. And he was selling them at school; not actually selling them himself, but getting the money from the sale, which was the same thing.

The headmaster walked back around to the other side of his desk and waited for Fred to answer, but when it became obvious that he was not going to speak the headmaster turned towards Joe.

"As Fred doesn't have anything to say to contradict your version of what happened, you may return to your lessons, Joe. If in future you find yourself in a similar position, you must do the right thing and refuse to do what you are asked. And you must report it to us immediately so that we can deal with it. We will not tolerate bullying at this school."

"Thank you, sir," said Joe, "but I don't think it will happen again."

"I wish I could be so sure," replied the head. "I sincerely hope so, but that will very much depend upon Fred here."

He moved his gaze from Joe back onto Fred and then back again. "You may return to class now, Joe."

And with that, Joe, staring down at his shoes checking to see if he'd trodden in some dog poo, turned and slunk off back to class.

"I've asked the deputy head to drive to your guardians to bring them here so we can discuss this further."

As if by magic, there was a knock at the door and in came the Deputy Head accompanied by Fred's aunt.

"Ah, Mrs. Floggit, thank you for coming so promptly. Do take a seat," said the head pointing to the armchair next to his desk.

Yes please, thought Fred, *do take a seat, Aunty Nora. I need one for upstairs in my bedroom.*

"No doubt, Mr. Brady, the deputy head has made you aware of the disgraceful display of bullying that Fred has perpetrated against a weaker member of his class?"

Aunty Nora turned towards Fred and gazed into his eyes as if hoping to find an open window into his mind with a dictionary open at the page containing the word 'perpetrated'. Failing to do this she wiggled her bottom in the chair and coughed nervously. Not knowing what to do next, she pretended she understood what the headmaster had said and waited for what else he might have to say that would give her a clue.

"I must tell you, Mrs. Floggit, as I have explained to Fred, the school takes bullying very seriously, very seriously indeed. It is for this reason that I have decided to suspend your nephew from attending this school for a whole week. Were another instance like this to occur in the future, I can assure you the consequences will be much more severe."

Following these words, a deafening silence fell upon the room. It was as if a poisoned mist had descended on everyone and they'd fallen into a state of sleep.

"That will be all," said the head breaking the spell. "You may take Fred home with you. I'm sure you will impress upon him the seriousness of what has happened, and see that it never recurs."

He paused and turned towards Fred.

"Is there anything you would like to say?"

I'd like to say the Chocolate Robin poem, thought Fred. And, seeing as you asked, I'd also like Aunty Nora to take you up on your offer of a chair. Given a choice I'd have yours, the one behind your desk, but on second thought, it might be too big to get up through the hole in the ceiling so I'll settle for the one aunty Nora is sitting in.

Luckily for Fred he kept his thoughts to himself.

"It was an unfortunate incident, sir," he replied, "and I, like Joe, am sure it will not occur again."

"I'm glad to hear that," said the head slightly taken aback. "Now, it's time for you to think about what you did and to make sure it never happens again. We'll see you back in school a week from today. Thank you again, Mrs. Floggit."

Chapter 23
What to Do Now

It was as if Chocolate Robin knew what was happening. As Fred and his aunt left the school, he was waiting outside and followed them as they set off into the nearby park.

"It's all a mistake, Aunty Nora," said Fred. "One of the boys wanted to sell some of my sweets and foolishly I let him. I didn't feel I could say no, for his uncle is going to make me some special boxes to put them in. The trouble is that when the boy got caught, he said it was all my idea and that I'd forced him to do it. The head took that as bullying."

"I hope you explained all that to the head," replied his aunt.

"How could I? It wouldn't have helped. It would have been my word against the other boy's. It was my fault for trusting him. I'll not do that again in a hurry. I've learned my lesson. I'll trust my own instincts in future."

Aunty Nora put her arm around Fred. It felt strange. He vaguely remembered his mother doing that to him when he was young, but it was too long ago now to be sure.

He stood up to break away from her embrace and bent down to give Chocolate Robin a stroke. "Aunty Nora," he said, "will you be daft and sing a song with me?"

"Oh, I'm hopeless at singing, Fred. Why don't you sing it to me?"

"I bet this dog is hopeless at singing too," replied Fred as if he'd never seen the dog before in his life. "Let's see if he is," and with that he lifted up Chocolate Robin's front paws and they danced around in a circle whilst Fred sung the Chocolate Robin song.

When you're feeling sad or gay
Turn around, then smile and say
Chocolate Robin!

"Isn't that strange?" said Aunty Nora. "I remember your father singing that when he was growing up. He thought it did magical things. I hope it brings you luck, Fred. You deserve it."

"Aunty," said Fred, "can you help me with something?"

"Of course, Fred. As long as you don't ask me to sing."

Setting up the bank account proved easier than Fred had imagined. Being too young to be able to use the account in his own name, they set it up under the control of his aunt. She was given the bank card but she happily gave it and its password to Fred once they were outside.

Fred explained to her that he wanted the account to keep the money he hoped to earn from selling his sweets. What he didn't tell her was how much he'd made already or what plans he had for the future.

Using some of the money he had on him, he took his aunt to the fish and chip restaurant for lunch.

"Wasn't that strange back there?" said his aunt. "Imagine that big dog let you pick up its front legs and dance with you. It was as if he was your dog."

After their meal, he escorted his aunt back home. He said he wouldn't come in for he wanted to be on his own and have a walk to think over a few things. Chocolate Robin was waiting for him a few yards up the lane. They set off for Mr. Marlow's.

"I think the sheep have done their job in the front garden. What do you say we take them up the road tonight and put them back in their field?"

He got a wag of a tail and a gentle woof for an answer, which he took as a yes.

"Fred," said Mr. Marlow, hurrying around from behind his counter, "come with me." He led Fred into a small room at the back of the shop.

"It's been quite a day. Word got around about our selling your sweets and we were inundated with people. We sold all the ones we bought off you this morning. A lot of people came in just to buy your sweets. They weren't interested in our meat. In the end, we put up a notice saying that people wishing to buy sweets must also buy meat. I think I'm in the wrong business. Your sweets are the thing!"

Mr. Marlow put his hand into the pocket of his overall and fished out a fat envelope. "Here's the money for the sweets I bought off you this morning. If you count it, you'll see there's more than we agreed. The sweets were so popular, I put up the prices and the customers still bought. It's only right that you should have some of that too. We'll have to sit down together and work out a strategy." He handed the money to Fred. "I thought you'd be all excited but you seem strangely sad. Is anything the matter?"

Fred opened his mouth to speak and then closed it again. This was neither the time nor the place to talk about it. "Another day," said Fred. "Perhaps we can talk another day."

"Another day it is, Fred. Another another day."

They smiled at Mr. Marlow's stupidity.

"Will you do me a favour, Mr. Marlow?" asked Fred. And not waiting for an answer, he continued, "Will you pay the money into my bank account? I don't want to carry a lot of money around with me. Even Chocolate Robin knows it's not a good idea."

"Of course, I will."

"Here's my account number. I opened it this morning with my aunt."

Mr. Marlow took the envelope of money back.

"I hope this will be the first of many deposits, Fred."

"I hope so too, Mr. Marlow… now if you'll excuse me, I'll be off. The headmaster has given me some time off school, which in a way is perfect for it will give me lots of time to make sweets."

"My son used to get extra time off school when he was your age. I'm sure everything will work out fine. I've got some empty egg boxes for you, you'll be needing them I'm sure."

Fred left the shop clutching a pile of egg boxes.

"I'll talk to you later," he shouted over the top of them. "Come on, Boy. We'll drop these off home, then we've shopping to do."

Chapter 24
Making Good Use of His Time

When Fred got back home, he unloaded his purchases in a heap alongside his bed. He wanted to sit down to think but the mattress on the floor had deflated and he couldn't be bothered to blow it up. He looked at his bedclothes and the pillow lying on top of them, just as he'd left them that morning. To give himself something to do, he took a stroll around his room.

Two paces to the left; ceiling. One pace to the right; ceiling. Two paces from the bottom of the bed; window. Two paces from the head of the bed; the ladder going downstairs.

"Prisoner 42, turn to the left!"

Fred paused for a moment then continued, "Quick march!" But knowing how close the ceiling was, he took care to not march quickly for fear of smacking his head against the roof.

"One, two, bump!"

"One, two, bump!"

Each time he did it, he pretended he'd banged his head on the ceiling and cried out, "Fire, police, ambulance!" and collapsed in a heap on the floor, holding an imaginary bump on his head.

"Prisoner 42; has anyone ever told you you're an idiot?"

"AND IF PRISONER, WHATEVER YOUR NUMBER IS, DOESN'T STOP MESSING ABOUT UP THERE," bellowed the prisoner in the room below, "I'LL COME UP AND GIVE YOU A GOOD THRASHING!"

"Fat chance of that happening," said Fred under his breath and laughed at his unintended use of the word fat.

Rolling onto his back, he spotted a spider in the corner of the room over by the window.

"I thought I'd got rid of all of you the other day," he said talking out loud. "How can you put up with sitting there all day waiting for something to happen? Why don't you get moving and make things happen? Go hunting for your prey, go out into the world, why wait for the world to come to you?"

Fred knew he wasn't really talking to the spider but to himself. He felt trapped and desperate. There was nowhere for him to go. There wasn't even a chair for him to sit on, and as for a table he could sit next to and write down his thoughts, however feeble, he could forget about that. Even if he had a table and a chair, he'd need a light to see what he was doing.

To cheer himself up, he slid down the ladder for fun, but again made a mess of his landing. With an almighty thud, he crashed into the living room door which luckily didn't burst open.

"I've had enough of this, Vera," screamed his uncle. "The only thing he's good for is cooking, and if I get my hands on him, I'll certainly cook him. I tell you he's got to go."

"Now, now, Arthur. It's not as bad as that."

"Oh yes, it is. I've a good mind to ring up that council lady who brought him here and tell her to take him away."

"You make it sound like he's a dustbin, Arthur. He's a boy. Do you not remember when you were a boy? Things happen when boys are around."

"That's just it, Vera. Things happen!! But I don't want things to happen. I want my peace and quiet back. He's in the way. I want him out of here."

Fred tried to ignore what was being said but, after being sent home from school, it only added to the weight on his shoulders. Slowly, he climbed back up the ladder and walked across to the window.

"Good luck with the rest of your day," he said to the spider as he passed, and he clambered out of the window and down into the garden.

Surprise surprise! Who should be waiting there but his friend, Chocolate Robin.

"I've had enough, Old Boy," he said as he sat down on the grass next to the dog. "I don't know what to do any more."

Fred idly ran his fingers through the dog's hair and wished he hadn't when they got all tangled.

"One day, we're going to have to give you a good bath; that is if I save up enough money to buy all the soap it will take."

Chocolate Robin turned his head and looked towards Fred.

"I'm luckier than you," Fred continued, too preoccupied with his thoughts to notice the dog dribbling on him. "At least, I get a shower after games at school each week. All you get is a good roll around in a dirty puddle after a downpour. You and Uncle Arthur should start a 'smelliest person in the world' competition'. It's hard to tell which of you would win."

Chocolate Robin got up suddenly to his feet.

"Sorry, Old Mate. That wasn't a nice thing for me to have said. You don't compare to Uncle Arthur!"

Chocolate Robin turned around, stretched his front legs forwards and arched his back.

"How do I get out of the mess I'm in?" asked Fred, preoccupied again with his thoughts. He looked up into the clouds as if expecting to find the answer written in them.

"Or should it be 'how do we get out of this?' for you're in a bit of a hole too."

As usual, Chocolate Robin didn't look concerned if he was in a hole or not.

"We need a plan," said Fred. "A grand plan. One that will not only solve the problems we're in today, but all our problems."

He imagined himself standing on the podium at the United Nations, announcing to all the countries of the world the incredible changes he was going to make to life on earth.

"Right," he said, "sitting around here all day won't get anything done. I announce, to everyone here listening—that's you by the way, Chocolate Robin—I'm going to make a huge success out of making sweets." And with that, he stood up, cupped his hands together, and blew through them like he would a trumpet.

"I can make money by doing what I'm doing, Chocolate Robin, but it is not enough to make a real change in my life. I have to find something that makes my sweets incredibly special. So special that whatever price I charge, everyone will still want to buy them. I need boxes like Joe's uncle makes, boxes that make them look like they're worth a million pounds, for the sweets inside will taste like a million pounds."

As he said these last words, he threw his arms into the air and almost decapitated Owlie who was flying in with another load of fungus in his beak. As it ducked to save its life, the bird dropped the fungus. It landed on Fred's head.

"That's it," cried Fred. "That could be the answer I'm looking for," and without explaining himself, he leapt to his feet and tripped over Chocolate Robin. He mumbled a quick "sorry, Old Mate", and scampered off and up the ladder.

He grabbed bundles of fungus off the frame of the attic window, shot across his bedroom, and climbed soundlessly down the ladder to the kitchen without disturbing Uncle Victor. He dumped the fungus in a heap next to the sink and turned the oven on.

"It's going to work, it's going to work," he repeated over and over. "I know it is going to work. Look how much Uncle Victor liked the taste of the fungus I slipped into his last meal. Perhaps this was what Owlie was trying to tell me all along. Perhaps this is the secret ingredient that will bring me success... I wonder if I should wash it first?

Chapter 25
It Can Only Be up from Here?

Not knowing how best to use the fungus, Fred mulled over a few ideas.

"I think the best thing to do with the weed," he chuntered, "is to cook it in the oven until it's crisp, then put it onto a cutting board, take a large knife... no, a hammer would be better... and imagine it's Joe!"

"On second thought," he continued, "I'll just grind it. If I start smashing it, I might wake up the fog horn in the front room; I think I'm in enough trouble for now."

Fred knew his stupid thought about Joe meant nothing. It was like a Tom and Jerry cartoon, so silly it made him smile. Making himself laugh or smile when things go wrong always made him feel better.

Joe, the class bully, was no different from any of the bullies he'd come across. When faced with a problem of their own, they run away. They might get something out of hurting others, but they don't like being hurt themselves. Fred wondered if Joe felt proud of himself for blaming everything on Fred and escaping being punished.

"The only pity is," said Fred stroking the beard he didn't have and renewing his chuntering, "I really like the boxes his uncle made for the sweets. They look expensive; first class. I need something that looks first class if I'm to get good prices for my sweets. I'll never get rich selling them wrapped in old egg boxes!"

Ten minutes into the cooking of the weed, Fred regretted having started. The smell was terrible. It smelled worse than rotting seaweed. Indeed, it smelled ten times worse than cooking seaweed in an oven full of cow dung. He didn't need a smoke detector to tell him he was in trouble, Uncle Victor did that.

"VERA," he bellowed. "What's that dreadful smell?"

"I expect it's just the local farmer spreading cow muck on the fields again, dear."

"Don't be silly, woman. That's worse than cow dung. Get on your feet and find out what it is before I die of suffocation."

Payback, thought Fred. *You don't like having some of your own medicine. That's how I feel, Uncle Victor, when I have to go into the front room to eat breakfast!*

Fred's mind was off again on one of its rambles. This time, it ended up back on the puzzle he'd never been able to solve since his arrival; how does Uncle Victor go to the toilet when he's trapped in there?

Luckily, Fred's mind moved off the subject and onto more pleasant things. He opened the cooker door and looked inside to see how the weed was doing.

"Fred?" The sudden sound of his aunt's voice next to him made him jump with fright. "What are you up to?"

"I'm cooking, aunty."

"I can see that. But what is it? It's making an awful stink. Your uncle is unhappy about it."

He didn't need his aunt to tell him that. His uncle's voice had gone up at least a couple of octaves; he now sounded like an African bull elephant with a thorn stuck in its foot. He could hear him banging on the living room door. By some miracle, he must have lifted himself up out of the sofa without the help of a crane.

The living room door opened a fraction and a round head, that you could have been forgiven for thinking was a ball of hot lava, appeared. The skin on the neck supporting it was puffing in and out like an over bloated bull frog, singing to attract a mate.

"He has to go, Nora. He has to go even if I have to drag him to the social services office by his ear."

In the short time Fred had lived with his aunt and uncle, he'd got used to his uncle's huffing and puffing. Trapped inside the front room as Uncle Victor most certainly was, Fred knew he was as safe as if he'd paid money to go and watch the tigers in a cage at the zoo.

"Try not to stress yourself, Victor. I'm having a look at what's going on. Sit yourself down. I'll bring you a nice cup of tea."

"But what is it you're cooking?" she asked whispering. "It smells dreadful. I hope you don't expect anyone to eat it."

"It's not a very nice smell, is it?" he replied, stating the obvious. "I don't think I'd want to eat it either, but Aunt, this is what I gave Uncle Victor yesterday, and he loved it!"

"Oh Fred," she said. "You mustn't do things like that. You could kill him. He is your uncle after all."

Aunty Nora was so upset she turned and left without having made her husband the cup of tea she'd promised.

"Oh Fred, I don't know what we are going to do with you."

She opened the living room door and whispered something to Uncle Victor that Fred couldn't hear and the noise from his uncle slowly diminished.

Gently closing the door behind her, she returned to the kitchen and watched as Fred picked up handfuls of the black, dried up weed and plonked them in the largest bowl he could find—the washing up bowl!

"What do you think, Aunty? Would a bit of washing up liquid improve the taste?"

He turned and looked towards his aunt hoping to see her smile. Her face didn't change. She simply stood and watched.

Fred picked up bundles of the weed and crushed and rubbed them with his hands until all that was left was a pile of black dust. Satisfied he couldn't make it any finer, he turned to his aunt.

"Wish me luck," he said, and licking his finger to make it wet he dipped it into the dust.

Iggily wiggily wonky woo,
I hope it's nice and not like poo!

he chanted as if reciting a spell. He raised his hand towards his mouth to taste the powder and, as he did so, his eyes instinctively shut like sharks' do as they bites their prey.

"Woweeeeee!" he exclaimed.

His exclamation flew out of his mouth and around the room like a blown-up balloon escaping from his fingers.

"Aunty Nora, you've got to taste this. It's amazing."

"I'll take your word for it Fred. Now I'll go and tell your uncle you've finished?"

"But I…"

He was going to say 'I haven't finished, I've loads more weed upstairs to cook', but before he had a chance to say it, she was gone.

Another time, thought Fred. *Another time! Best not push my luck. I've plenty here to be getting on with for now.*

And with that, he started putting together the ingredients for his normal sweets, wondering, as he did so, how much of the dust from the weed he should mix with it.

Chapter 26
Next

The following morning, Fred rose early. He left a note for his aunt to tell her he would be out for breakfast and that he would miss Uncle Victor's delightful aroma (he didn't actually write the last bit, but he smiled at the thought of doing so). Setting off at a brisk pace, he took a sample of his latest sweets to test them out on Mr. Marlow.

During the night, Owlie had been hard at work. So much so Fred had difficulty getting out past the window for all the bundles of weed his friend had draped over it. Without a moment's thought, he picked up armfuls of the slimy mass and dumped them on the floor next to his unmade bed.

As usual, Chocolate Robin was waiting for him at the base of the ladder. Although he was in a hurry, Fred took the time to wrap his arms around him and give him a hug.

"Do you know, Old Boy, I don't know what I would do without you. I think you're the best friend I never had. You always seem to be there when I need you."

Without thinking, he tried to run his hands through the dog's hair but his fingers quickly got stuck in all the tangles.

"We're going to have to do something about your hair. What do you say we give you that bath?"

Chocolate Robin must have had other things to do that morning for without answering, he set off at a brisk walk in the direction of the garden gate.

"Perhaps we could cut all your hair off?" called out Fred as his friend, apparently in a big hurry, bounded over the branches that formed the garden gate. "Why don't we shear you like the farmers do their sheep?" he continued.

But by this time, Chocolate Robin was too far away to hear.

"I thought we'd go to see Mr. Marlow," said Fred, when finally he caught up, "but then, something tells me you knew that already."

"Good morning, Fred," said the butcher. "I've got something for you."

"And I've got something for you," replied Fred.

"Let me go first," said Mr Marlow. "I think you'll want to hear this."

The butcher took Fred through the shop to a small sitting room at the back.

"A man came in yesterday and asked me to show you these."

Mr. Marlow went over to a small table in the corner of the room, picked up some highly coloured pieces of card and gave them to Fred.

"He gave me his business card. He said you'd know who he was. He said he was the uncle of that boy who got you into trouble at school."

Fred's first reaction was to hand the pieces of card back to Mr. Marlow and tell him that if Joe had anything to do with it, he wasn't interested. But when he saw the decoration printed on the pieces of card, he knew he couldn't do that. This had nothing to do with Joe. This was business between himself and a printer; someone who just happened to be Joe's uncle.

Fred's eye was drawn to a picture of an old English sheep dog that was printed on each card. Unlike Chocolate Robin, it was a clean English sheep dog sitting upright and alert, lively yet relaxed and calm, as if something good was about to happen.

"I like them, Mr. Marlow. They make you want to pick them up and buy them."

"That's what I thought, Fred. Perhaps I should get some to wrap my meat in!"

Fred felt so happy, he wanted to rush outside and tell Chocolate Robin, but he turned to the butcher instead.

"This packaging is just what my business needs, Trevor."

Fred felt himself pause as he became aware that he'd called the butcher by his first name. He thought of correcting himself by saying Mr. Marlow but realised that would have sounded strange for he wasn't talking to Mr. Marlow the butcher, he was talking to a friend he was in business with.

"They're just what I was looking for," he said, brimming over with pride.

"Now it's my turn to surprise you. I want you to taste a few of the sweets I made yesterday and tell me what you think."

He carefully cleared away the boxes Joe's uncle had given to Mr. Marlow and placed four sweets of different flavours in a line, on the table.

"Please don't tell me what you think until you've tasted them all, Mr. Marlow," said Fred deciding that after all it would be more polite and respectful to address the butcher by his family name. "I only want to know what you think at the very end."

The butcher picked up the first sweet and tasted it. Like an expert tasting wine, he only took a small piece and moved it around slowly inside his mouth. When he thought he'd tasted enough, he took it out of his mouth with a piece of tissue paper and placed it to one side.

"Number one," he said.

He repeated the process with the second, then the third, placing each on the table next to the one before, counting each one out as he did so. He gave away no indication of what he thought. When he finished tasting all four of them, he sat back.

"Before I give you my opinion, Fred, I'd like to say something first."

The muscles on Fred's arms and legs began to tighten and his tummy rumbled.

"People know me as an honest man, Fred; someone who, if they ask me to give them an opinion, know I will always tell them exactly what I think. I will make no exception for you. You have asked me for my opinion and, like it or not, that's what I'll give you.

"I don't want to disappoint you," he continued, "for I can tell by your excitement that you are expecting me to notice something different about them, something remarkable even."

Fred could feel Mr. Marlow's embarrassment building up as he spoke.

"But I can't see what's different. They're all lovely and I'd happily buy any of them, especially the marmite flavoured one. And I'd quite happily sell them for you; as many as you'll give me. But I can't see what's changed or why you asked me to taste them."

Sunshine came through the window and illuminated the table. They looked each other in the eyes. Mr. Marlow was trying to search for a clue in Fred's face but found none. Showing no emotion, Fred picked up a fifth sweet, put it on the table, and looked at the butcher.

The butcher hunched his shoulders as if to say 'OK, I'll play the game' and picked up the fifth sweet. Exactly as he did with the other four sweets, he broke off a small piece and, with all the enthusiasm of someone who has lost interest in a game, he popped it into his mouth.

"My word," he cried. "What have you done?"

Fred showed no emotion as he gazed into the butcher's face trying to read the expression written on it. Had he liked the taste, or had he not? He thought he'd liked it, but perhaps that was just because Fred wanted him to?

Each second he waited, passed like an age.

Mr. Marlow's lips remained tightly shut but his cheeks moved in and out as his tongue manipulated the sweet from one side of his mouth to the other. He was enjoying the sweet so much, he forgot it was a tasting test he was doing and that he should take the sweet out.

"Forgive me," he said coming up for air. "But I'm not wasting that one. Whatever you've done, Lad, you're a winner. That taste was unbelievable! I've never tasted anything so delicious!"

The butcher's words ran away with themselves.

"You've made the caviar of sweets! A truffle, a black truffle," he added as an afterthought. "But who cares! Whatever food you liken it to, it tastes expensive, gourmet, special, posh! Fred, you're a master. You're a winner. Here, let me taste another one just to check," he said with a cheeky smile on his face. "It would be a waste really, but let's see what the customers think."

Fred handed the butcher another sweet which they broke into small pieces. Mr. Marlow put them on a plate and placed it on the counter of the shop.

"And a lamb chop for you, my boy," he said as he took the meat outside and gave it to Chocolate Robin. "Not good to eat between meals, but then nor is eating sweets."

He turned and went back into the shop. "Kevin," he said speaking to his son, "I want you to look after the shop on your own today. Fred and I have to talk business!"

Chapter 27
A Whirlwind

Fred and Mr. Marlow spent the rest of the day discussing how Fred might set up a business. Together with Aunty Vera, they went to visit a lawyer who suggested they form something called a partnership in which Fred, Mr. Marlow, Aunty Nora, and everyone who worked in the business would have a share in its success. The lawyer explained how well it worked in a famous big shop and, because Fred liked the idea of everyone having a share in the business, he decided that this was what he would like to do.

He was to own 80% in something called a Trust, which would be held for him by his aunt until he was old enough. Mr. Marlow and his aunt would each have 5%. The remaining 10% would be shared between the employees. Chocolate Robin was named as one of the employees though he showed no interest when Fred explained it to him.

The old man, who owned the shop next door to the butcher, decided to retire so Mr. Marlow agreed to rent it off him. They converted it into a sweet shop with a kitchen at the back for doing the manufacturing.

It took quite a bit of money to set the shop up in exactly the way Fred wanted and, because the bank wouldn't take the risk of loaning them the money to do it, Mr. Marlow took some of his savings for his retirement and loaned it to the partnership.

Later that week, whilst they were working on the shop, Joe knocked at the door. He looked ill at ease. He came to apologise to Fred for what had happened at school. He said he'd learned his lesson and that he'd never do anything like that again. For the first time in his life, he'd come to understand the meaning of friendship.

As it happened, Joe had no need to say what he said for it was written in his expression and Fred knew that he meant it. He went over to Joe and thanked him for what he'd said for he knew how difficult it must have been for him to say it.

"I'll see you in school on Monday, Joe, and we'll catch up on everything that's happening."

Aunty Nora was delighted for Fred that he'd set up the business but was frightened in case it all went wrong and he lost everything.

In a short space of time, a big change had taken place in Fred's life; coming to live with his aunt and uncle; seeing their poverty; his bedroom; the rats; his start at the new school and being suspended for a week. So many of them had been difficult. But they were behind him now and he had much to look forward to.

And let's not forget Chocolate Robin; never a word to say but always there, like a rock; giving him support. How much Fred's life had changed since he'd wandered into it, and how much he'd learned since he'd been there.

As for Owlie?

Throughout the time Fred spent with Mr. Marlow setting up the business, Owlie worked hard collecting fungus from high in the trees. And he too formed a partnership of sorts. He organised a mini flock of owls to help him do the collecting and carry the weed, so much so that by the end of each day, the bedroom window was so festooned with weed, it was on the point of collapsing.

Now that the cooking of the fungus was done at the back of the shop, Uncle Victor had one less thing to complain about and as time went on, he calmed down a bit.

The biggest surprise came from Chocolate Robin.

One day, he turned up at the shop with another Old English sheep dog alongside him; a clean one with gleaming hair beautifully combed. Fred couldn't tell, and Chocolate

Robin never said, but he guessed it was Chocolate Robin's girlfriend.

Seeing them arrive, Fred rushed out to greet them. The girlfriend's hair was smooth and soft and smelt of violets, which was more than he could say about Chocolate Robin's.

"We must do something about your hair, you know, Old Boy. What do you say we get some of Mr. Marlow's meat knives and cut it all off?"

Things began to go well at school too.

On the Monday, Fred went back. He was called in to see the headmaster and given another boring lecture free of charge. But no lecture was needed. Fred had already decided to settle down and work hard in school, which he did with some success.

It was no surprise to anyone that he decided to call the shop 'Chocolate Robin', and it was not long before the big London shops heard about the amazing taste of their sweets and sent buyers down to negotiate contracts to buy them.

Aunty Nora started to work in the shop and loved every minute it. Left on his own at home, Uncle Victor got tired of shouting to himself. Bored by his own company he couldn't wait for Aunty Nora to return and, hard though it may be to imagine, he almost became reasonable.

Fred built a large kennel at the back of the house for Chocolate Robin to sleep in, and had a heater fitted to keep him warm in winter.

It was while they were building the kennel that Chocolate Robin sprung another surprise.

Unannounced, he marched into the garden and started barking. Wondering what was the matter, they turned to look as in through the open garden gate walked his girlfriend and 6 tiny balls of fluff.

"Congratulations, Old Mate!" said Fred. "That's a lovely family you have there."

Fred raised his hand up to his face and began to stroke his chin thoughtfully. "From the look of them," he continued, "I'd say the three with clean shiny hair are girls and the others…"

He paused for effect.

"I'm not sure how to put this… the boys look just like you!"

If Fred hadn't known better, he'd have sworn Chocolate Robin nodded his head in agreement.